The Spider Wars

Lizard World,
Book Three
Raptor's Tooth

A Science Fiction novel
By
Herbert Grosshans

Published by
Melange Books, LLC
White Bear Lake, MN 55110
www.melange-books.com

The Spider Wars, Lizard World, Book 3 Raptor's Tooth,
Herbert Grosshans,
Copyright © 2011

ISBN: 978-1-61235-261-9

Credits

Copy Editor: Sherry Der Wille
Line Editor: Mae Powers
Format Editor: Mae Powers
Cover Artist: A.Bratt

The Spider Wars - Lizard World
Book Three, Raptor's Tooth

A Science Fiction novel
By Herbert Grosshans

Visit Herbert's website:

http://hegro.shawwebspace.ca
http://hegro.blogspot.com/

Works also by and including Herbert Grosshans:
Outpost Epsilon
Orola, Warrior Priestess
Seeds of Chaos, Books 1 and 2
Web of Conspiracy Trilogy
Stars in Chains, Books 1 and 2
Stardogs 1 & 2
The Xandra Trilogy
Cliffs of Time
Orion the Hunt
Beyond the Stars Digest
Orion: Symbiont of Passion
Men of Eros
The Spider Wars, Books 1 & 2

Chapter One

Of all the different denizens inhabiting Epsilon, the *Boraz* was by far the most docile but also the dumbest. At least according to Gilbert Turner, who was trying unsuccessfully to free the unfortunate struggling creature. As large and as strong as a donkey, it was an ideal pack and riding animal. With its large webbed feet, it could move with ease across swampy areas, of which there were many in this jungle of mushrooms and tall ferns.

"How can you be so stupid and get yourself entangled in a Spider-beetle net?" Turner shouted at the unlucky recipient of his anger. "It's getting late and I'd like to be back in the shelter before dark."

He had set up his small portable habitat a few miles back near the spot where he found some nice-sized sapphires. According to the terrain, there should be more such spots in this area.

The Boraz stopped struggling for a moment and looked at him out of large brown eyes, as if to say *I'm sorry*.

"Don't look at me like that," Turner grumbled. Walking around the giant net, he studied its construction. It looked old, abandoned. Lucky for the Boraz, otherwise the owner of the net would have made an appearance by now, and the beast would provide a small family of Spider-beetles with a tasty snack.

Turner knelt and peered into the deep hole under the net and listened. He didn't hear anything and was satisfied with his assessment of the hole's vacant state. The situation didn't look hopeless, but if the Boraz fell into it, all Turner's gear would be lost in the dark depth of the abandoned shaft. In the unlikely event the Boraz survived the fall, he'd need a rope to climb to the bottom, but the needed rope was stored away in one of the packs on the animal's back.

The struggling Boraz dislodged some of the debris the net had collected over time, and Turner discovered remnants of bleached skeletons from other unlucky victims who had stumbled into the web. Gingerly, he touched a strand and noted most of the sticky substance had dried up. With luck, he should be able to pull the Boraz back to the safety of solid ground.

I should have carried my most important stuff in a backpack. Serves me right for being so careless.

Anything could happen in these wild areas of Epsilon. This wasn't the first time he lost one of his pack animals. But it was the first time he would lose two of them on one trip. The Boraz, which he had been riding, made a quick meal for one of the carnosaurs a few days ago while he was preoccupied digging for *Moth-eggs*.

Taking stock of what he carried on his person, he found he still had his hunting knife, his flash rifle, his pistol, his water purifier, and his helmet with its air filter and built-in headlamp. Luckily, he carried his torchlight and his first-aid kit clicked into his belt and his navigation equipment strapped to his wrist. He would not perish or get lost should he lose the Boraz with all his other possessions.

He looked up and stared through the mushroom umbrellas, noting the blue sky. At least the weather co-operated and he might even get lucky and make it back to his shelter without needing his rain-gear should that eventuality happen.

The Boraz let out a loud bleeping cry and began struggling again.

"Don't make so much noise," Turner hissed. "We don't want to advertise our presence to every carnosaur in the vicinity."

But, of course, the animal didn't understand the severity of the situation and, at the moment, it desired nothing more than to be free of its restraint. Turner noticed one of its webbed feet had broken through the tough strands of the net and realized the material lost its elasticity and may not be able to support the weight of the struggling animal for much longer. Already, some of the strands had ripped loose from their anchors in the rim of the nest.

He searched for something he could use to help him with his task.

Dammit! If only I had the rope. I could throw a loop around his head and pull him to safety. Of course, I might just strangle him in the process. Something I feel like doing right now anyway.

"I can't believe your stupidity!" he cursed, partially at himself and partially at his unlucky companion.

A rumbling roar made him jump. Then he looked around for a place to hide. He knew he didn't have much time. That had sounded too close to be ignored. A guest was about to drop in for a visit and he didn't want to be around to greet him.

He remembered seeing an entrance to a cave in the cliffs they passed only moments before the Boraz managed to trap itself in the net. Fortunately, the cliffs were in the opposite direction of the approaching carnosaur and within sight. He threw one last look at his soon-to-be ex-companion, feeling sorry for the poor creature. Then he sprinted toward the cliffs.

Glancing back over his shoulder, he saw the large predator appear among the ferns, the great head with its gleaming teeth moving from side to side as it surveyed the small clearing. It roared again when it spotted the frantically struggling Boraz and sauntered toward its next meal.

Turner reached his destination and entered the, what he hoped, protection of the cave. There was no guarantee some other vicious and inhospitable beast didn't occupy his new hiding place, but he could deal with that eventuality later. Right now, he was happy to have escaped becoming a snack for the large predator eying the wailing creature in the Spider-beetle net.

Turner should be safe. The entrance to the cave was barely large enough to let a Human squeeze through. Fortunately, Turner had never been on the chubby side or he might have found himself in a tight spot. Literally.

Even though nobody challenged his entering the dark interior of the cave, he wasn't fooled by that. He had learned in five years of prospecting on Epsilon never to take anything for granted. His life could depend on it.

He removed his pistol from its holster and unclipped the torchlight from his belt. Then he searched his new surroundings. The cave was not large, but there was an opening in the back, and when he shone his light into it, he saw a narrow tunnel leading farther into the mountain. Anything could be hiding behind the tunnel.

Satisfied he didn't face any immediate threats, he turned back to the entrance and peered outside, just in time to see the giant carnosaur lean forward and sink its long teeth into the writhing, struggling body of the Boraz. The little creature gave one last shriek before the great lizard pierced it with its dagger-long teeth.

The scientists had named this particular specimen Rex, after its long extinct cousin on Earth. The similarity between the two species was uncanny, except this one was apparently somewhat smaller than Tyrannosaurus Rex. Something Turner disputed, seeing the size of the one devouring his unlucky pack animal.

He shuddered as he watched the huge beast tearing the Boraz apart with its teeth and claws.

That could be me if it weren't for this cave.

Seeing the packs that contained his possessions ripped open and trampled under the beast's huge hind feet, he cursed silently. He could afford the loss of the Boraz, but his possessions were a different story. Some of the stuff was hard to get. He couldn't just walk into a supply store and purchase anything he needed. There weren't any stores on Epsilon, except for the trading posts in Star City or Epsilon City, a thousand miles to the south. At that, it was questionable if he would be able to buy everything he needed as a prospector.

"Son of a bitch!" he cursed under his breath. One of the bags contained a few nice-sized sapphires. They would have bought him many supplies, maybe even a scooter.

The Rex lifted its huge head and seemed to listen intently. Turner became aware of a low droning sound coming from somewhere above. He stuck his head out of the cave entrance and searched the sky. The droning increased in volume, and then he saw a large shadow crossing the openings between the mushroom umbrellas obscuring the sky.

He recognized the shape immediately and, without thinking, he stepped out of the cave, oblivious of the Rex for a careless moment.

A shuttle. He wondered about the sound it had produced. Normally, the shuttles only emitted a barely audible humming.

Something must be wrong with this one.

He brought his attention back to the huge carnosaur as it roared loudly and began advancing toward him with a speed belying the bulk of the animal. He barely managed to jump back into the cave when the huge shadow of the Rex blocked the entrance, and then the front part of the toothy maw poked into the cave.

Turner pressed his body flat against the back wall, his flash rifle ready, in case the giant predator managed to enlarge the entrance hole with its armored forehead. The small confines of the cave amplified the rumbling roar of the Rex, and Turner couldn't help but feel terrified.

The impulse to fire his rifle into the row of flashing teeth was strong, but he suppressed it. Burning off the head of the Rex would kill it, but it would serve no purpose other than attracting more predators. He'd still be trapped inside the cave. Possibly for days.

No, that was not the answer. The only thing he could do was to wait for the Rex to get tired of gnashing its teeth and finally depart to hunt for easier prey.

Maybe he could encourage the angry beast to leave. He pulled out his gun and put an impact-bullet into the scaly nose. The sound of the discharging gun and the exploding bullet nearly burst his eardrums.

With a roar, the Rex withdrew. Encouraged by his success, Turner fired another shot, smiling grimly. This particular specimen wouldn't be able to smell anything for quite some time, but eventually, the destroyed part of the nose would grow back again. He could hear the enraged carnosaur thrashing outside, but he didn't leave his spot in the rear of the cave, in case the beast decided to try one more time to get at the morsel within apparent easy reach.

Finally, the noise seemed to move away from Turner's hiding place, and then it was gone. Cautiously, he poked his head out of the cave entrance. When he was certain the Rex had actually left, he sat down, his back against the rough wall, and relaxed.

He would give it some time before he'd venture outside. This cave was as safe a place as he could hope to find. He played the beam of his torchlight again across the walls and floor to make certain none of the small, possibly poisonous critters were waiting for an opportunity to sink their fangs or stingers into his unsuspecting exposed body parts.

The reflection from an object on the floor caught his eye. He focused the light on it and was surprised to discover a number of black, glittering balls the size of child's fist in front of the entrance to the tunnel that led into the interior of the cliff.

He picked up one and studied it. It looked and felt like crystal. Its smooth surface and perfectly round shape almost made him think this was not a natural product but something artificial, something someone had made. As he held it in his hand, he felt a slight tingling sensation traveling up his arm. More prove that this was not a naturally occurring object.

But who made it? None of the intelligent races Humans had discovered so far on Epsilon had the technology to make this.

He collected the remaining balls and stuffed them into his pockets. They were surprisingly light. He would have to study them at a more appropriate time. Maybe even try to break one open to see what it contained inside.

Deciding it was time to leave the safety of the cave, he stepped outside.

There wasn't much left of the Boraz. A few bones, a tiny piece of its knobby tail, and the short horn from its forehead were the only evidence it ever existed. But Turner almost whooped with joy when he found three of the sapphires and one of the packs nearly intact. It must have dislodged itself when the Rex yanked the Boraz from its prison.

Not all was lost.

Still cautious, he scanned the surrounding forest and listened for unusual noises. Sometimes these beasts liked to lie in hiding, waiting for an unwary victim, but the normal clatter of small animals living in the ferns and mushrooms was coming back to life and he knew the Rex had left for good.

Remembering the shuttle that had passed overhead, he again wondered about the strange droning sound. If it had engine problems, it might have landed nearby, or even crashed. He groped in his pockets for a *Seeker* and pulled out the marble-sized robotic spy-eye. Activating it by linking its tiny terminal for a short period with his *Nav-Comp* strapped to his wrist, he waited until it glowed brightly, and then he disconnected it and threw it into the air.

Should the shuttle be nearby, it would find it and transmit its location to his NC.

The thrashing of the Boraz had destroyed most of the Spider-beetle net covering the tunnel that led into the abandoned nest underground. He knelt and peered into the darkness below, wondering what creatures still called it home. Sometimes *Ghost-scorpions* would live side by side with the Beetles. Silent and deadly, they had a habit of jumping on top of their intended prey and stabbing a poisonous stinger into the victim's belly.

Epsilon was not a place for cowards and careless travelers. One had to be on guard at all times, eyes open and weapons ready…preferably a flash rifle and a detonation device.

Life on Epsilon was hard and one wondered why Humans bothered to live on this harsh planet. Turner asked himself that question for the umpteenth time as he studied his surroundings. He knew why he came to Epsilon. Getting here had been easy; leaving was the difficult part nobody warned him against.

Huge mushrooms rose into the sky, their wide umbrellas shading the ground from the sun. Tree-like ferns and other vegetation grew around the thick mushroom stems, and blue-shimmering moss covered rocks and most of the soft ground. The unpleasant odor of decaying plants mixed with the stench of the carnosaur's mountain of fresh feces invaded his nostrils, suggesting he should be breathing through his air filters.

Large and small insects buzzed everywhere, trying to find a place to land on his body to either sting him or suck some of his blood. The electronic repeller he wore around his neck prevented them from doing so, but he found the constant buzzing irritating.

Even though the mushrooms kept the sun's rays away from the ground, the air inside the forest was uncomfortably hot and stifling. The high humidity plastered his clothing against his skin, causing a nearly irresistible urge to loosen his collar.

He cursed silently. The loss of the Boraz was more than inconvenient. With it he could have made it back to his base before nightfall. Inside his habitat he could have taken off his clothing and dried his body without worrying about insects eating him alive.

A soft beeping sound made him check the tiny screen on his NC. The *Seeker* had found something. Taking a reading, he noted whatever the little spy-eye detected was not far away. Only about ten miles north from his position. He should be able to reach it before dark.

* * * *

Turner cursed under his breath and swatted at a large *Dung Wasp* that insisted on circling in front of his face. He missed, but the irritating insect seemed to get the hint. It buzzed away but not before spraying his hand with a streak of yellow mist.

Turner wiped his hand on his pants, grateful the insect's parting gift was not poisonous, even though it stung for a moment.

He put his field glasses against his eyes again and went back to watching the scene in the small valley below.

Hiding in the protection of an outcrop of boulders, he felt safe from being discovered by predators who might wander through the area and confident the objects of his study would not become aware of him.

At first, he had been elated when he came upon the shuttle and ready to run into the valley, but experience taught him caution. As far as he knew, these people could be criminals, outlaws, or worse, alien renegades.

He adjusted the zoom to get a closer look at the three people walking around the shuttle. They seemed to be studying their landing place. One of them carried an instrument, which he used to scan the moss-covered ground.

Turner could see a swamp nearby but they didn't seem to be interested in it.

"Wonder what they're searching for," he murmured.

The three people looked humanoid, but he was certain that no human engineer had designed the shuttle. Too many angles and crazy curves.

Although he was eager and anxious to go down and introduce himself, he suppressed the urge. Something didn't feel right. For one thing, he didn't believe the shuttle had crashed. It didn't appear to be damaged, and those three crewmembers didn't act worried or distressed.

He'd spend the night hidden among the rocks. Maybe by morning things would look different.

The mushroom umbrellas were obscuring the sun, but he knew it was close to dusk. He looked at his timepiece and realized nearly half an hour had passed since the bright ball of the primary disappeared behind the tops of the mushrooms. Soon it would be dark. The darkness brought the night creatures, the Bloodfrogs among them. He was happy not to be too close to the swamp, a favorite hiding place of the Bloodfrogs and Bullfish.

The absence of leafy plant tops above him exposed him to predators from the air, but so far, he hadn't seen any Dragons, Eagles, or any of the other larger winged carnivores.

After one last look at the shuttle, he was about to move further back among the boulders, when he heard the low droning sound of another approaching vessel. It appeared high above the mushroom umbrellas to his left and sank swiftly, heading in the direction of the shuttle on the ground.

Craning his neck to get a better look, Turner whistled softly. He had no doubt Humans never designed or built the new arrival either. As it settled softly onto the hard ground, long spidery stabilizers appeared in the vessel's sides.

Then it squatted silently on the blue-green moss, like an ugly giant black bug. Or more precisely…a giant spider.

Turner shuddered involuntarily and pressed his body closer to the ground. Maybe he shouldn't move at all. He had no idea what sophisticated detection devices they had on their ship.

Humans knew virtually nothing about the Spiders. To his knowledge no Human had ever been on any of their ships. At least none who lived to tell.

He stared at the alien shuttle, his heart pounding. This craft should not be here. The Spiders had no business on Epsilon. In fact, they had no business to be in this star system at all. The Spiders shunned the Humans, ignored them mostly, keeping contact to a minimum. It seemed Humans had nothing they wanted.

As he watched, a hole appeared in the side of the Spider vessel. From it swarmed a horde of hairy, long-legged creatures. At least to Turner it seemed like a horde. When he counted them, he found there were exactly twelve. They had oval shaped bodies, about three feet in length, but with their six long legs, they appeared large, tall, and menacing. He could see sharp mandibles moving rapidly as they surveyed their surroundings.

In addition to their six legs, they also possessed two shorter front limbs, which clearly served as arms. Turner saw what looked like tools or possibly weapons held by long, bony fingers.

The three humanoid figures started walking toward the horde of Spiders. Turner didn't see any hostility between the two groups when they met by the alien ship. He couldn't hear them but he knew they were communicating with each other.

He zoomed in on one of the Humanoids and let out a surprised grunt.

A woman. She had long blond hair, tied into a loose ponytail behind her head. No question, she was a Human. And beautiful too.

Her two companions were males. Also Humans.

Now what kind of business would three Humans have with a horde of Spiders? On Epsilon, of all places.

This did not look good and it was not something he could afford to ignore. He groped around in his pack and was satisfied when he found his small camera. Then he recorded the meeting of these two dissimilar groups. Unfortunately, he couldn't record their conversation. He was too far away for that and the built-in microphone was not sensitive enough to pick it up at this distance. Aside from the fact there was too much noise all around him. Too bad, it might have been interesting to hear what they talked about.

He felt a sudden and strong urge to get away from this place. As fast as possible.

Darkness descended swiftly, and as soon as he felt it was safe to move without fear of being detected, he began crawling back toward the protection of the jungle. Protection in this case was only a relative term. He'd be protected from the ones in the valley but not from the predators who would be roaming the night.

He remembered the empty half shell of a giant *Rocksnail* he saw at the edge of the jungle before he came upon the clearing. He hoped he could find it in the dark. It would provide adequate protection for the night.

When he reached the safety of the thick ferns, he switched on his torchlight and kept it dimmed but bright enough to see where he was going. Unfortunately, the light also attracted insects and other annoying critters.

He found the shell, made certain no one else had decided to use it as a home, and then he crawled under it. Sighing, he adjusted his electronic insect repeller and made himself comfortable.

Living on Epsilon was treacherous and full of danger, but he was used to it. After spending years traveling through hostile jungle, swamps, and burning deserts, he had learned to make use of any shelter this world offered. Surviving was not that difficult for a man who knew where to look and what to expect.

Feeling secure in his temporary shelter, he slept quite peacefully through most of the night. When morning came, he decided to take a chance and check out the intruders in the valley one last time.

Moving as fast as he could, he wormed his way back to the large boulders. Lying on his belly, he took a careful look and received a great surprise. The Spiders had been busy during the night.

Turner stared at the structure protruding from the moss-covered ground.

Bubble-shaped, with a diameter of at least one hundred feet and a height of thirty it could be mistaken for one of the Human habitats, except the material the Spiders used was alien and something Turner had never seen before.

The surface of the bubble glittered and sparkled with a multitude of colors in the rays of the morning sun. The Spiders were still busy with its construction.

Zooming in on one of the Spiders, Turner saw a fine strand coming out the Spider's body as he swiftly moved across the surface of the shell, laying the strand over it.

This is incredible. They are spinning it. It seems the strands harden as they are exposed to the air.

Counting the scurrying Spiders, he realized there were at least twenty of them spinning a tight web layer by layer. Surprised by their number, he looked around and soon discovered another Spider-ship beside the first one. It was about twice the size of the other ship. He didn't see any of the Humans, but their shuttle still stood in its place.

Looks like they're digging in. I have a feeling things are about to change on Epsilon.

When he studied the Spiders going about their task, he noticed that the newcomers were different from the first dozen he had seen. These were gray, whereas the first ones had been black. The newcomers were also much larger and bulkier.

The construction crew, I assume. Might be a good idea to file this information away for future reference.

A few of the black Spiders had spread out in the area surrounding their new structure. Turner was quite interested in the objects they carried in their long-fingered hands. They looked suspiciously like energy rifles.

Turner's assumption proved correct when a large carnosaur appeared out of the thicket. It sauntered toward the Spiders, expecting an easy meal, but it didn't get far. A burst from one of the energy rifles sliced it neatly in half.

Turner shuttered watching the two chunks of carnosaur meat toppling to the ground. The extreme heat of the raw energy had cauterized the wounds, keeping the blood from leaking out and the entrails from spilling onto the rocks. He could see the giant head still snapping, while the powerful hind legs on the severed lower half kicked up the blue moss. It would take a while for the small brain to realize its owner was dead and for the muscles powering the legs and claws to calm down.

"A Human wouldn't stand a chance against such a weapon," he muttered. "I think I'll make myself scarce."

The fact that he didn't see any of the Humans around, hastened his decision to leave. For all he knew, they could be exploring the immediate area around their campsite to make sure no uninvited guests dropped in. His chances of being discovered were high.

He took a few more pictures. Then he crawled back toward the jungle. Suddenly, the ferns and mushrooms with all their potentially dangerous inhabitants seemed like a safe sanctuary.

When the thick vegetation of the jungle closed in around him, he breathed a sigh of relief. Rising, he secured the pack around his shoulders and began the long trek back to base camp.

He still wondered about the reason the Spiders were setting up a habitat on Epsilon. Could they be dinosaur hunters? Anything was possible but somehow he doubted that. There had to be another explanation for their presence here.

Chapter Two

There were no straight trails in the mushroom jungle. When Turner was lucky enough to find one that led in the direction he headed, he followed it, but most of the time he had to use his machete to cut a path. Fortunately, the undergrowth was not so thick to make moving through it impossible, but progress was slow.

He missed the Boraz. With its armored head and chest a Boraz moved with great efficiency through even dense vegetation, making traveling so much easier. And with its webbed feet it moved easily through swamps and even small lakes. With the animal's absence his small habitat was suddenly too far away to reach in even one day. Now he had to walk around one huge swampy area through unfamiliar territory.

At midday, he shot a small *chicken* and rested for an hour, during which time he roasted strips of the dark meat. Wolfing them down, he realized he hadn't eaten since the day before.

That evening, he slept inside a ring of dead thorn bushes. The normally bright-red color had faded to dull brown, and the razor-sharp thorns were not as hard and pointy anymore, but they still offered excellent protection against the night-creatures. Even though quite sure it didn't house any *Fire-spitters*, he had made certain of it. Those huge-headed serpents could inflict great pain with their wads of acid-spit.

Early morning brought rain. It poured for over an hour, making it impossible for him to move on, so he stayed in his shelter, curled up, and feeling miserable without his raingear and the company of the Boraz.

Digging for gems and spending time in the jungle for weeks, sometimes months, was a lonely task, and he found himself on occasion talking to no one in particular just to hear a human voice. Having another living being as companion helped to fend off the feeling of foolishness, even if that companion was only a dumb animal.

"Why did you have to go and stumble into a Spider-beetle net?" he mumbled. Running his hand across his beard, he felt the sudden need to shave and take a bath. The clothes he wore were rainproof and didn't let any water through. He pulled the hood of his shirt over his head to keep the water from running down his collar, but the humid air plastered his shirt and pants against his body.

The rain stopped and he could see the sunshine breaking through the mushroom umbrellas. He was about to crawl into the open, when he heard loud rumbling from a reptilian throat. Lying still, he watched one of the great carnosaurs appear among the mushroom stems. It wasn't a Rex, only one of its smaller cousins, but equally ferocious. It stopped and swung its huge head from side to side, surveying the area with sharp glittering eyes. Two rows of razor teeth gleamed between powerful jaws, ready to sink into an unwary victim.

Turner didn't know the scientific name for this one, but it didn't matter which of these huge reptiles gobbled him up if he were caught between those dagger-long teeth. He kept perfectly still, even held his breath, in case the carnivore's keen sense of hearing picked up the fluttering noise the dry thorn bush leaves might make as he breathed across them.

It finally moved on. Its long thick tail brushed the branches of the bush Turner lay under, almost touching him. Turner waited for a few more minutes after the giant carnosaur was out of sight before he moved. Cautiously looking around him, he rose, shouldered his pack, and carried his flash rifle in his hands, ready to be used. The huge animal left a trail in its passing and Turner decided it was safe to use it since it led in the direction he traveled.

By midmorning, the sky darkened again and he could feel the wind picking up speed. It blew from the south, and when he inhaled the foul smell of *devil's spores*, he realized that traveling any further was impossible. He snapped the air filter over his face to keep out the toxic spores. They wouldn't kill him, but inhaling the spores of *Lucifer's Fungus* would cause him to hallucinate, making him see things that weren't there.

One had to be extremely lucky to survive that. A carnosaur might appear as a cuddly and playful huge dog, and the flower of the *Iris of Venus*, a meat-eating plant, took on the shape of a beautiful woman.

He used his machete to cut a swath away from the trail and began heading west in hopes of skirting the explosion of the spores. He had never been this far up north and the region was unknown territory for him. Apparently, the area further west was home to a nation of *Fire-Ants*, the Eer, who supposedly were hostile to visitors. As far as he knew, they had never had contact with Humans and might consider him prey. As it was, Humans had only a loose relationship with the Uur, the nation near Epsilon City, but at least they were peaceful, which could not be said for the Eer. They were supposed to be a warlike race.

Only his extreme caution saved him from discovery. The glint of a number of large chitinous bodies moving through the thicket stopped him from advancing further down the trail. He knew they were *Fire-Ants* when he saw the bright-red heads with their long, black antennas. They moved silently in single file, like a company of soldiers marching into war.

Most likely hunters on their way to their favorite hunting grounds, Turner thought. He noticed the long spears they carried. The movement of their black antennas told him they were communicating with each other. The Ants didn't have vocal cords. Instead of using a voice box they used their minds to speak to each other.

He didn't have to worry they might read his mind. Supposedly, they were not telepaths who could pick up his thoughts at random, not the hunters and workers. The class of queens and nobles was different from the common members. They'd be able to look into his mind and make him do and see anything they chose to.

At least, that's how it was with the Uur. He expected the *Fire-Ants* to be the same way, but then again…he could be wrong. The Eer were still unknown to the Humans. Everyone knew they existed, but nobody knew anything about their customs and abilities.

He waited until they disappeared from view before he moved on. After traveling another hour, he stepped out of the jungle into a huge area bare of mushrooms. The rocky ground was covered with sparse low growing shrubbery and lichen. Then he saw the giant dome reaching into the sky and he knew this was the home of the Eer. It meant the end of his journey in this direction.

Before he could make up his mind which way to go, his ears picked up the sound of something moving across the hard ground…something slithering at fast speed, and it seemed to be heading in his direction. When he saw the long, serpentine body moving toward him, he recognized it immediately.

A Sandserpent.

Hard scales on the thick, sinuous body shimmered blue, reflecting the bright light of the sun. Curved plates gleamed red on the massive, triangular head; open jaws revealed white fangs and a long forked tongue.

Houston stared into the yellow glowing eyes and wondered for a brief moment if the poison the serpent's bite injected into his bloodstream would act as a painkiller or if he would feel the pain when the dagger-long fangs pierced his chest.

Then his adrenalin kicked in and his body sprung into action. With one fluid motion he let his flash rifle flow into his hands and, lifting it, he aimed it at the gaping maw. As if recognizing the danger, the giant snakehead dipped lower and his first bolt of energy went astray. Roaring a challenge, the great serpent slithered closer at an alarming speed, moving erratically from side to side. Even though it presented a large target, it was not easy to get a fix on the fast-moving body.

This time he aimed at a spot below the weaving head, but missed again. After that, things happened so fast, he could barely remember what exactly took place. Realizing, he wouldn't be able to hit the serpent in time, he threw himself to one side. Something hard slammed into his hip and he fell, rolling away as he hit the ground. His flash rifle was torn from his hands; his face scraped the hard rock. Dazed for a moment, he tried to crawl away, but a heavy weight pressed his body onto the rocks below him.

He steeled himself for the excruciating pain when the long, muscular body of the serpent would coil around him and crush his chest, but it didn't happen. The body of his attacker convulsed and kicked him aside. He heard a hissing roar that was cut off with a sudden rushing sound, like air escaping from a giant balloon. He lay on his belly, trying to catch his breath, when hard hands dug into his arms and pulled him away from the thrashing body of the serpent. He rolled onto his back and stared at his rescuers.

Glittering multifaceted eyes looked down on him out of red, hard-shelled faces.

Fire Ants.

When he moved his head, he saw the massive body of the Sandserpent lying lifeless beside him. A group of Eer was already busy cutting it into chunks with their sharp mandibles. Others stood watching them, spears in their three-fingered hands.

Two of his rescuers were still standing above him. Sitting up, he winced when a dull pain radiated from his hip. He looked up into the immobile red faces of the two Fire Ants and gave them a friendly smile, hoping they didn't interpret it as a hostile act. "I don't know if you can understand me but thank you. I thought for sure I was going to end up in the belly of that hungry lizard without legs."

Their faces didn't give him any clues as to what he could expect next. He hoped they didn't view him as just another trophy to be added to their daily meat supply. "If you don't mind, I'd like to stand up."

He rose slowly to his feet. The two Eer moved back a little to make room for him. He stood and brushed the dust from his clothing. His body ached from his encounter with the hard rocky ground and his nose and face stung. "I hope I didn't break my nose," he said, probing his face with his fingers.

They didn't comment on anything and he didn't expect any comments. The Eer, like the Uur, their cousins, weren't equipped to utter sounds.

"By the way, my name is Gilbert Turner. Gil to my friends. I hope I can count on you as friends. The fact that you saved me from certain death is a good sign…I think. Maybe some day I can return the favor." His eyes fell on his flash rifle, which lay not far from him. "Would you mind if I get my rifle? I promise I won't use it against you. I might need it in the future for my protection." He chuckled. "Not that it helped me much against this beast."

He walked over to pick up his weapon and gained back some of his confidence when they didn't stop him. Adjusting his backpack, he shouldered his rifle. "If you don't mind, I think I'll keep on moving. I'm just passing through." He began to walk away, but one of the two Eer stepped into his path. Then it pointed in the direction of the giant hive.

"You want me to come with you? Is that it?" Turner shrugged. "Why didn't you say so in the first place? Maybe we can have cookies and tea together. Perhaps swap stories." He knew he was chattering to cover his anxiety. If he could at least see some emotion in their faces, but the only mobile part in their faces were their black lips and they didn't even quiver to show some sort of reaction to his babbling.

The rest of the Eer seemed to have finished their task. They picked up huge chunks of the serpent meat and began walking toward the cone, each one carrying a load as large as its body.

Turner walked between the two who had pulled him to safety. It was a long walk to the hive. The closer they came to the tall cone, the larger it seemed to become. The region around the hive was busy with Eer going about their business. Turner noticed some groups cleaning up debris, while others seemed to do nothing.

"I guess you have loafers just like we have in our society," he commented, but he didn't believe the ones he saw were actual loafers. They were doing something that was not obvious to him. Some of them carried spears, like the two who walked on either side of him, and he assumed that they were probably guards or warriors.

They were headed for an oval hole in the hive. It was not as large as the entrance to the hives of the Uur…the ones he had seen. A number of guards with spears stood on either side of the entrance. One of Turner's two companions stopped to converse with the guards for a short time, while the group carrying the meat walked right in.

The inside of the Eer hive wasn't much different from the hives of the Uur. A tunnel with a dirt-packed road led into the interior and wound itself toward the top of the hive. Secondary tunnels split from the main tunnel, leading to separate rooms and compartments in which the family units resided…if they had families.

Of course, Turner didn't know anything about the social life and structure of the Eer society, but he assumed it was similar to the Uur.

The tunnel was lit by softly glowing points on the ceiling and on the walls. He recognized them as *glimmer-mushrooms*. They weren't exactly poisonous, but consuming them produced hallucinations, not all of them pleasant. He made a point of reminding himself not to nibble on any no matter how hungry he'd get.

The ones carrying the meat had disappeared into a tunnel. Only the warriors walked with him.

"I hope it isn't too far," Turner said to his two closest companions. "My hip is aching fiercely. I should take something for the pain."

They didn't answer. He would have been surprised had they actually made some kind of a reply. "Don't answer if you don't want to," he said, chuckling a little. "I know you can't because of your lack of a vocal cord, but maybe you guys are different. Maybe you have some kind of voice box that allows you to make sounds."

When they finally took a side tunnel, he hoped they had arrived at their destination, wherever it was. The group stopped in front of an oval hole in the wall. One of them pointed.

Turner hesitated, not sure what he was supposed to do. When the other warrior gave him a gentle nudge toward the opening, he shrugged. "I guess you want me to go in there," he said. "I hope it's not an oven or a meat smoker." Stepping into the space beyond the hole, he found himself in a small room. A couple of glimmer-mushrooms on the ceiling didn't throw much light, leaving the room in near darkness. Switching on his headlamp, he looked around the bare room and murmured, "So this is what a Fire-Ant jail looks like. At least it's cool in here."

He took a few breaths, sniffing the air. "A little stale," he said, just to hear a voice, finding the silence eerie and disturbing. "Maybe their air-conditioning broke down."

He leaned his rifle against the wall and shrugged off his pack, letting it slide to the ground. Unclipping his first-aid kit from his belt, he searched for a painkiller. As the tiny pill slowly dissolved under his tongue, he felt the effect almost immediately. The pain in his hip subsided and so did the slight humming in his head caused by smashing it against the hard ground.

Then he sat down with his back against the wall, switched off his headlamp and waited. Tired from his ordeal and from the long walk, he closed his eyes and tried to relax. He felt safe in his cell, quite confident in the assumption that if his captors wanted him dead, he would be dead now.

He didn't know how long he sat waiting. Hearing a soft scraping sound, he looked toward the opening and saw the outlines of one of the Fire Ants blocking the brighter light from the corridor. His visitor climbed into the room and looked down upon him with its multifaceted eyes. Then it touched him on the shoulder and gave him a slight push toward the door.

Turner rose from his sitting position and walked ahead of the Eer into the corridor. Outside the room, the large creature took the lead, indicating with one arm that he should follow. The corridor was busy with Eer walking in different directions and Turner wondered what jobs they performed. He followed his guide back into the main tunnel. Once on the wider road, they took the direction leading toward the top.

Except for the clicking of mandibles it was eerily silent inside the hive. No voices, no laughter, the way it would have been had Humans occupied the hive. The sounds from the jungle didn't penetrate the walls. The only other noise came from the scraping feet of the groups of Eer walking along the road that wound its way through the giant structure. He felt a slight breeze on his skin, indication the hive had an efficient air circulation system. When he sniffed the air, he found it fresh and pleasantly cool.

The painkiller he had taken, masked most of the pain in his hip, but he found it increasingly difficult to keep up with the Eer walking ahead of him. "I hope we'll be there soon," he said, his words echoing from the silent walls. "You might have to carry me."

As if it understood him, his guide stopped and waited for him to catch up. Then it turned into one of the side tunnels. It ended abruptly. The tunnel was darker than the one they left. When Turner's eyes adjusted to the light level, he noticed a curtain made from woven fibers covering an oval hole in front of him. His guide pulled the curtain aside and made a gesture with its hand, pointing at the hole.

Turner walked by the Eer and entered the room behind the hole. He noted that his guide did not follow him.

The room he stepped into was not well-lit. He discovered it was actually only a wide tunnel that led deeper into the dark interior. Carefully, he walked ahead in the semi-darkness, refraining from switching on his headlamp and wondering what waited for him. He missed the assurance of his flash rifle and his sidearm. Both were back in his prison cell.

It was warm and moist in the tunnel, and when he inhaled he detected a sweet smell in the air. His advance came to a sudden halt when two large dark shadows loomed in front of him. He stopped and waited for them to make a move, but they stood like two immobile statues blocking his way.

"I was told to come in here," he said. His voice sounded hollow in the confinements of the corridor. "I am not armed and I harbor no ill will to anyone." He felt foolish talking to creatures that obviously didn't understand him, probably didn't even hear his words, but he needed to talk just to stay sane.

Something touched his mind, like ghostly, spidery tendrils of smoke, searching…searching…

You would not be here if it were otherwise. The words sounded loud and clear, but he knew it was only an illusion. They had not been uttered by vocal cords. The creature had spoken to him with its mind.

He took a deep breath. "You can understand me?"

Yes.

"Why are you keeping me prisoner?"

Your question will be answered. Come with us.

He knew it would be useless to ask more questions. Shrugging, he followed the two Eer down the corridor. When it ended, he found himself in a larger room. Looking around, he saw a number of Eer moving along the walls. The walls were dotted from the bottom to the top with round holes. He saw movement in the holes and when he looked closer, he realized what he saw where the heads of young Eer. The heads were small and pale, the multifaceted eyes colorless, probably blind. Open mouths gaped and snapped, obviously demanding food. Their undeveloped mandibles opened and closed uselessly, creating a soft hissing sound.

The adult Eer by the walls were feeding the young from containers they carried in front of them. He realized this must be a nursery.

Turner's escorts took him through more rooms filled with breeding compartments before they ended up in another large room. This one was different from what he had seen so far; in its center stood a contraption that looked like a bed made from reeds. On it reclined one of the Eer.

As Turner stepped closer, he was surprised by the size of the creature. It was nearly twice as large as any Eer he had seen till now. A few smaller Eer sat on either side of the bed on cushions made from some unknown soft material.

The Eer on the bed regarded him silently out of glittering eyes. Its black antennas weaved like a couple of serpents back and forth. The large mandibles opened and closed with slow rhythmic movements.

Turner had a hunch that he probably stood in the presence of a member of the Royal cast, if they had the same social structure as their cousins, the Uur. He made a little bow, hoping it was the correct gesture. "I am honored to meet you," he said.

A sound like laughter ringing through his mind made him look at the creature in surprise. "Did I say something that strikes you as humorous?" he asked. He deducted a creature that knew how to laugh must have a sense of humor.

I am intrigued by you, Human.

"Why?"

You are soft-shelled and yet you wander through a hostile environment without the protection of a squad of warriors or even in the company of others of your kind. I am told you stood against one of the Legless ones. Are you a warrior or a hunter?

"I am not a warrior but you could call me a hunter."

What do you hunt? Surely not the great scaly beasts?

"I am not that kind of a hunter. I am searching for gemstones." He knew the Eer would read the meaning in his mind.

Why are you searching for those?

He shrugged. "There are individuals of my kind who value them for their beauty."

You find them beautiful? That is something I cannot understand.

"The Uur mine them. They make jewelry out of the gems and trade with the Humans."

We have avoided the Humans, but we are aware of your presence. We have been watching you from a distance. You are not from our world.

"No. We come from the stars, from another world."

How did you get here?

"We came inside giant husks called spaceships."

I do not understand that, but from your mind I see that you speak the truth. What do you want on our world?

"We are looking for places to live on. Our world is becoming overcrowded."

I do not understand that either. How can a world become overcrowded? It seems to me your world has lost its balance.

He was surprised by the Eer's words. This was not a stupid giant bug. The Eer may appear as savage, primitive creatures, but they, like the Uur, had a sophisticated society and they were thinking individuals. "It probably has," he agreed. "Humans are not the only ones who have outgrown their birthplace. There are many other races out there among the stars that have done the same thing. All are looking for more *Lebensraum.*"

Are they all coming here to our world?

"I hope not. Some are but your world is quite hostile and not suited for most of them. I don't think any, including us Humans, will ever flourish on this world."

There was a pause as the Eer seemed to ponder his words. After a while it said, *We would never allow anyone to take away our world.*

"May I ask what position you hold in your hive?"

Again the silent laughter. *I am the Queen.*

Turner took another bow. "I am pleased to meet you, Your Majesty."

You have a strange way of expressing yourself, but I understand the meaning of your words.

"Can I ask you a question? I couldn't help but notice all those young Eer. Are they all your children?"

My children? The Queen's surprise was evident. *No, they are not. They belong to the Mothers who have been designated to breed. I am the Queen. My designation is to be the Ruler of this hive.*

"You have no offspring of your own?"

I have ten daughters. They are Secondary Queens with their own sections in the hive, but I am the Supreme Queen. She moved her body into a different position and seemed to study him intently with her huge glittering eyes.

"What are your plans for me, Your Majesty? Am I a prisoner?"

No, you are not my prisoner. I have no plans for you...not yet. At least none that I can think of at the moment. When I was told of your presence I was curious about you. You are free to leave, but answer my question...what is your reason for coming to our hive?

"I am on my way to my hive. I never had any intentions of trespassing into your territory. I apologize for that." He smiled, even though he knew she probably didn't know what a smile meant since the Eer couldn't show expressions with their immobile faces. "I was a bit worried when your warriors took me into your hive. According to our information, you are a warlike race."

If by warlike you mean we will defend our territory then you are correct, but we do not attack others without being provoked.

"I am glad to hear that," Turner said. "I will let my people know you are not an aggressive species, but that they should respect your right to the area you occupy."

Tell your people we wish to be left alone. If we want to communicate with you it will be under our terms.

"I appreciate you telling me that. We do not seek war with anyone on this world." He hesitated. "I have discovered people from another world who may not be as peaceful as we Humans. Perhaps your warriors should take care if they run across them on their hunting expeditions. They are setting up a base not far from here. I am trying to get home to my people so I can warn them."

Then you must leave soon, but it is nearing darkness and traveling in the shadow of the dark god is more dangerous than traveling when the shining goddess rules. I suggest you stay in our hive until the Lightgiver shows you the way.

"I accept your offer with gratitude, your Majesty, even though I am in a hurry to get home to my people," Turner said. He had to admit he was tired from the ordeal with the Sandserpent and his body ached. A good night's rest in the safety of the hive would be welcome. He looked at the queen with searching eyes. "Did you want me to go back to the room your warriors put me in? If so, I'm afraid I don't know the way back."

You are my guest. I am inviting you to spend the cycle of dark here in my chambers.

"What about my things I left behind in the room? My food is in my backpack."

I will have one of my workers bring them.

"Thank you. I am most grateful for your hospitality." He looked around. "Where did you want me to sleep?"

I will have a place prepared for you.

"One more favor. I am quite thirsty. Would you have some water I could drink?"

Not water but I can offer you some of the nectar we feed our brood. It will not harm you.

He wasn't quite sure about that, but when one of the workers came and handed him a bowl filled with a sweet-smelling liquid, he sniffed it first and then he took a tiny sip. It tasted surprisingly like honey and he drank it slowly. "It is good," he said after emptying the cup, hoping he

27

wouldn't suffer from any unpleasant side effects. But then he figured Humans have been eating bee honey for thousands of years on Earth. There was no reason his system shouldn't be able to absorb the honey from the Eer…at least that's what he told himself.

Come join me on my bed and tell me more about your people, the queen told him.

He stepped closer and sat down at the edge of the bed. The queen touched his chest with a long finger. *You feel soft. Is your whole body this soft?*

He laughed. "I'm afraid so."

Why are you covering your body with more soft material?

"For protection against poisonous insects, against injuries from thorn bushes, the weather, and for other reasons. In my society people don't usually walk around in the nude. We call it *modesty*." He chuckled. "Don't ask me to explain that."

But it does not protect you from hard blows. I could push my fingers easily into your body, causing you great injury.

"Yes, you could, but I hope you won't. You could kill me."

She pulled on his beard. *Is this part of your body?*

"Yes. It is called a beard…it is made up of hair." He took off his helmet and let it drop to the floor. "I have hair on my head and on other parts of my body. It grows and sometimes I cut it shorter. Usually I shave off my beard."

Why?

"It makes me feel more civilized. Some men let their beards and hair grow for different reasons. It is a personal preference for some, a religious requirement for others. Don't ask me to explain."

Remove your covering. I am curious to see how you look underneath it.

Her request came as a surprise, but then he shrugged and began slipping out of his clothing. When he stood naked in front of the queen, she gingerly touched his body with one hand and let it trail down his chest. Her hand felt warm and soft on his skin. It slid across his belly. When she reached his genitals, her three fingers curled around his penis.

Is that your productive organ?

"Yes, it is." He laughed, somewhat embarrassed by her forward question and her hand on his genital. He became even more self-conscious when his penis reacted to her touch.

Why is it getting hard?

"It is a natural response to your touch," he explained, feeling uncomfortable when he noticed the other Eer watching with apparent great interest.

Does that mean you want to copulate with me?

"I don't believe that would be possible," he said. "You and I are of two different species. Your body is hard while mine is soft."

Your productive organ is not much different from that of our males. She took his hand and pulled it toward her lower body. *Touch me. Not everything on my body is hard. Some parts are only hard on one side.*

What he touched felt soft underneath his fingers. Soft and warm. She pulled his hand down across what would have been a human woman's belly, down to where her legs were joined to her body, until his fingers touched a swollen mound, softer yet than her belly. When he moved his fingers they entered a moist slit. He pulled back his hand as if he had touched something hot and unpleasant, knowing fully what he had encountered.

Her laughter sounded amused and almost teasing in his mind. *Does touching my female organ repulse you?*

He didn't know what to say, feeling more embarrassed than ever before. Especially since his penis strutted like a hard mast away from his body…for all the watching Eer to see. They couldn't be so ignorant as not to realize that he was beginning to feel extremely horny.

His head felt a little dizzy and a hot flush rippled through his body, most of the heat concentrating in his lower region. He suspected there had been more in the sweet nectar than fruit juice. "No, it doesn't repulse me," he managed to say. "It surprised me."

Do you Humans copulate only for propagation or do you copulate also for pleasure? Again her question surprised him.

The throbbing in his loins pulsed in rhythm with his beating heart while his penis seemed on fire. "We copulate mainly for pleasure," he moaned, "when we get the chance. Without the pleasure the human race probably would have faded out of existence by now."

Lie down beside me.

Like a puppet on a string he obeyed and joined the queen on the wide bed. As he lay beside her, her fingers curled again around his stiff organ and pulled him closer. Under her guiding hand, his penis touched her soft lower body. He didn't resist when a pair of wet, strong muscles grabbed the tip of his organ and sucked it into a hot moist sheath. Pushing forward, he groaned loudly as soft walls molded tightly around his rigid member. Forgetting his surroundings, he snapped his pelvis back and forth in the female Insectoid's embrace, like a mindless automaton, bent only on spilling his seed into the milking vessel keeping him prisoner inside its hot inferno. He lost all sense of time, just kept thrusting in and out…in and out…

* * * *

When he regained his senses, he remembered little of what had transpired. His head felt heavy and his body exhausted, drained, as if he just spent hours cutting a swath through dense jungle with his machete.

He lay on a wide bed made from reeds. Alone.

Looking around in the semidarkness, he saw a number of Eer sitting near the bed, watching him with their multifaceted eyes. He sat up and rubbed his forehead. Pieces of memory, like bits of a dream, flashed through his mind…

Lying on his back, he watched the dark shadow of the Eer-queen moving slowly above him. He couldn't make out her features clearly against the dark ceiling, but he felt the soft pressure of her sex-organ around his penis as he swam in a sea of pure rapture that left his head spinning, unable to form clear thoughts…

"What the Hell was in that drink they gave me?" he murmured. "Did I really have sex with the queen or was it just wishful thinking? I feel so tired I need another day to recuperate. Next time I'll refuse these welcome drinks. Wonder what time it is?"

When he looked at his watch, he realized he was completely naked, except for the watch strapped to his wrist. His clothes lay in an untidy heap beside the bed. The tiny screen on his watch showed five a.m. It had been late afternoon when the queen called him into her chambers. How long had he coupled with her? How many hours did he sleep? Not many according to the way he felt.

Getting off the bed, he picked up his clothes from the floor and put them on. Then he saw his backpack on one end of the bed. At least the queen told him the truth when she said she'd have his things brought to him. Even his sidearm and his flash rifle were there.

The silence in the room was in a way unnerving. He was used to the noises of the jungle…during the day and during the night. It was part of his environment. Silence typically meant there was danger nearby, usually of the toothy kind.

His legs felt wobbly. He needed to rest before he entered the hostile world of the jungle again. When he lay back on the bed none of the watching Eer gave any signs of protest, so he closed his eyes, hoping to sleep for at least another couple of hours. He knew he was safe in the protection of the hive.

When he woke again, the watching Eer were still sitting around his bed, but he also saw movement along one of the walls where a few Eer were busy feeding the young sticking their pale heads out of their incubation holes. The light in the room seemed brighter than before. He became aware of the hissing noise the crudely formed clicking mandibles of the young Eer created.

When he checked his watch he discovered it was almost ten o'clock. He had slept without waking for nearly five hours. When he sat up, he felt much better; still a bit weak in the legs, but he was able to think clear thoughts. A gnawing in his belly demanded food. Pulling his backpack closer, he rummaged around in it and found a couple of energy tablets he'd been saving for an emergency. He swallowed one, and it didn't take long before he felt the effects.

Sliding his feet off the bed, he stood up and stretched. When he heard the footsteps of an approaching Eer, he turned and looked expectantly at the tall, bulky figure walking toward him.

I trust you have regained your strength? The queen's voice inside his head seemed to mock him.

He gave her a crooked grin. "I feel much better. Thank you."

The males of the Eer will couple with me as long as I request it. Many cycles of the Lightgiver if I demand it of them.

"Human males unfortunately do not have such stamina, I'm afraid. Once we spill our seed we have to spend some time recuperating before we can go on." He shrugged, chuckling. "It probably is a good thing, otherwise our home world would have been overpopulated a long time ago." A thought popped into his mind. "Tell me, when you make…um…offspring, how many young does a female of your species have?"

A female may lay as many as ten eggs.

"Ten eggs? Do they all hatch?"

Usually.

"I'm surprised your hive isn't crowded beyond capacity with all those children being born."

He detected puzzlement in her mental touch. *I can see from your thoughts that you do not quite understand our species. Only designated breeders will produce fertilized eggs. Not every female in our hive is able to lay fertilized eggs. Is that not so with you Humans?*

"No. Our females do not lay eggs. Our young are born fully developed. As a rule only one child is born, sometimes two or on rare occasions more, however all of the females from my species have the ability to reproduce. Even though the central government of my people's home world Earth made laws allowing only one child per family, there are many who did not obey those laws, and slowly the planet became overpopulated. Only the exploration of other worlds helped to ease the problem of overcrowding."

He didn't know if she understood everything he told her. Her species was so different from his. He didn't know anything about hers, but in a way it was probably easier for him to grasp the way her society worked than her understanding of his world.

She surprised him with her words. *Perhaps your species is not as far advanced or as civilized as you believe. To be able to control the population of a nation is part of evolving. A long time ago our ancestors were out of control and they spread across large areas of our world, but they changed and devised ways to keep the number of new hatchlings down. This hive will never be overpopulated. We will never have to leave our world to encroach on the living space of others.*

"You are probably correct when you talk about my world not being as civilized as we Humans think it is," he agreed. "I've never been on the birth world of the human race, but I know the history of Earth. There was a time, before Humans began exploring the stars, when countries, whose governments had the foresight, voluntarily cut down on the number of children because they foresaw the crisis over-breeding would cause, like food shortages, lack of sanitation, not enough clean drinking water, and other problems. Most citizens obeyed the laws, even though some religions did not allow birth control. The countries where the people already lived in poor conditions did not practice birth control. Couples, and often single women, had many children, sometimes more than ten, which they could not feed or take care of. Many died of starvation or sicknesses, while their parents died of sexually transmitted diseases." He sighed. "No, those people could not be called civilized. They were as ignorant as their ancestors thousands of years ago."

It seems to me your race has still much to learn. She had come closer to him as he talked. Her antennas quivered on top of her head and her mandibles clicked softly. *I must apologize to you for taking advantage of your vulnerable condition.*

"What do you mean?"

The nectar I offered you…it contained a substance that made you yield to my demands, but I was curious to experience what if feels like to copulate with a male from another species. From your mind I received the impression that you would be easy to stimulate. He could almost hear her chuckle in his mind. *And I was correct in the assumption.*

"I suspected as much." He looked into her immobile face. "I don't carry a grudge. It was a pleasurable experience."

I am pleased you feel that way. I also enjoyed our joining. Let me offer you nourishment before you leave us. Her soft laughter echoed through his mind. *Do not worry. It is just that…nourishment. It will give you strength and help to heal injuries you may have suffered from the encounter with the Legless one.*

One of the other Eer came forward and held out a bowl to Turner. He took it with some reluctance, but he decided to trust the queen. Swallowing the warm thick liquid slowly he let it soothe his parched throat. He handed the empty bowl back to the Eer and said, "Thank you." Picking up his gun-belt and holster, he strapped it around his waist and put his helmet on his head. Then he shouldered his pack and slung his flash rifle across one shoulder.

He looked around the room and at the silently watching queen. "I guess I'll be leaving now. If you would be so kind and lend me an escort to guide me out of your hive, I would greatly appreciate it."

I will have my warriors guide you safely to the spot where they found you.

A moment later four Eer with spears entered the room and stood waiting.

The queen stepped close to Turner and touched his cheek with one of her mandibles. It was a gentle touch, almost like the touch of a lover. *Travel with care. The Scaly Ones are hungry.*

He lifted his hand and curled his fingers around the claw. "I will remember the kindness you have shown and your good will toward me."

He smiled, knowing she would interpret it correctly. "I will also remember the softness of your body and the pleasure I found in our coupling." Letting go of her claw, he turned and looked at the four warriors. When they walked toward the exit out of the queen's chambers he followed them.

Walking down the road was much easier and he was surprised he didn't feel any pain in his body. He was full of energy and looked forward to resume his journey home.

The four Eer warriors accompanied him to the spot where he encountered the Sandserpent. They lifted their spears in a farewell gesture and walked back to their hive without waiting for him to make up his mind which way to go. When he searched the ground for evidence of his encounter with the serpentine beast, he didn't find anything to indicate a battle had been fought here.

He shook himself. Without the interference of the Eer warriors he most likely would have ended up in the belly of the giant snake.

Carefully, he traced his way back into the jungle. Then he made a decision. He couldn't travel directly south because of the *devil's spores*. There'd be a forest of *Lucifer's Fungus* in that direction. His air filters would not be able to prevent all of the spores from entering his lungs. Traveling east was also not possible. He knew from maps he would have to cross a giant swamp and a huge lake. He had only one chance to survive…the Humans he saw with the Spiders. He only assumed they may be renegades. Maybe they were traders who made a connection with the Spider race. Maybe he could buy their help with the sapphires in his backpack. If they were smugglers, they'd be able to get the gems off planet and be inclined to make a trade.

Turning north, he walked for about two hours, his eyes and ears open, wary of anything that might prove dangerous. Getting tired, he decided to take a break. There was no need to hurry. He wouldn't make it to the Spider camp before dark anyway. He found a nest of *Rootbeetles* under a clump of ferns and roasted them over a small fire. A few slices of edible fungus made lunch just about a gourmet meal. Instead of drinking the stale water from his canteen, he sucked the juice from a *Fernapple,* and he felt almost happy and satisfied with his life.

Almost.

He realized he was lost. For some reason his compass had stopped working. As long as the sun was visible through the umbrella roof, he could use it for orientation, but it would not be accurate. However, he didn't despair. He had been in tougher situations before. He could only hope his luck would not leave him.

Traveling in a northerly direction until it became too dark to move on, he looked for shelter and found it in the base of one of the giant mushroom trees. A crack, large enough to let him squat comfortably, provided enough protection from his hostile environment.

He kept his flash rifle on his knees, just in case, and he managed to get a good night's rest, as cramped as his quarters were.

The next day he sent one of his *Seekers* to search for the alien shuttle. Should he be close to it, the little spy-eye would locate it. He wasn't disappointed. The location of the Spider base was displayed on the small screen on his wrist. With renewed vigor, he carried on, in the direction the little spy-eye indicated.

He reached the base by nightfall. Debating if she should wait until morning and spend the night under the half shell of the *Rocksnail* or ask for help before it became too dark, he decided in favor of the latter.

This time, he didn't approach the aliens with stealth but walked boldly into the open. Maybe it was best if they spotted him before he reached the newly erected habitat.

When he came to the spot where he observed them days earlier, he stopped for a quick moment to survey his destination. He saw only the larger of the Spider ships and the shuttle the humanoids had arrived in. The other Spider ship seemed to have left.

Aware of the flash rifle in his hands, he hid it among the rocks. It wouldn't make a good impression to walk into the camp of strangers he intended to ask for help while carrying a rifle. He still had his pistol, should the need arise to defend himself.

Squaring his shoulders and balancing his pack, he climbed down into the valley.

About halfway down, one of the humanoids stepped from the shuttle and watched him coming closer. Turner saw that it was one of the males. Detecting no hostility in the man's posture, he relaxed and advanced slowly with hands spread and away from his body.

"I need your help," he called to the man, not knowing if he would be understood.

The stranger didn't say anything until Turner was close enough to make out the man's features. He looked young, clean-shaven…and human.

"Welcome to our camp," the man said, smiling friendly. "How did you find us here in this wilderness?"

Turner relaxed and stopped walking. "Pure chance and maybe a great deal of luck," he said. "I'm a prospector. My problems started when my pack animal got itself tangled up in a Spider-beetle net and eaten by a Rex…"

The man laughed. "Slow down. You can tell us everything in the safety of our shuttle." He looked around as the harsh bellow of a night-hunter in the jungle echoed through the valley. "I think we'd better get inside."

Turner sighed and exhaled slowly, his apprehension fading. "I agree."

Chapter Three

Even though the shuttle of the strangers had an unusual shape, inside, it didn't look much different from any shuttle Turner had been on. The instrument panel seemed unfamiliar, a new design perhaps, but nothing else looked out of place.

The woman gave Turner a smile when he stepped into the large cabin that served as the crew's living quarters. He couldn't help but notice her extreme beauty. She was tall, muscular looking but with almost excessive feminine features. Her large breasts strained against the thin fabric of her uniform.

The second man was lounging in a leather chair, studying a handheld computer screen. He looked up and tipped his forehead with his closed fist...the salutation of the Belters. Turner returned the gesture.

"I'm sorry to barge in on you this late in the day," Turner said. "But it seems I need your help."

The man behind him laughed. "Apparently, his pack animal was eaten by a Rex."

The other man and the woman joined in his laughter. "That's very unfortunate," the woman said.

"Unfortunate, indeed," Turner said. "It put me into an unpleasant situation. When I tried to get back to my camp, I got sidetracked by a storm that blew devil's spores into my face. After that I ran into a bunch of Fire-Ants, and then I got myself lost." He grinned lopsidedly. "I know it sounds like a ridiculous story, but it happens to be the truth." He left out the part where he spent time inside the Fire-Ant hive and his encounter with the Ant queen. That would have sounded even less believable.

"What are you doing out here in the jungle all by yourself anyway?" the woman asked.

"I'm a prospector." He shrugged. "Been trying to get lucky for five years."

"Ever get lucky?" The man in the chair took his eyes off the screen he'd been scrutinizing and looked at Turner.

"This planet is not a friendly place. It seems once you're stuck here it won't let you leave again," Turner said, his voice resigned. "How about you people? Mind if I ask what your business is on Epsilon?" He hesitated. "That habitat out there. I'm curious. What is your relationship with the Spiders?"

Turner didn't miss the slight narrowing of the man's eyes. He spread his hands. "Maybe I shouldn't have asked. It's really none of my business." He chuckled. "Who am I to query you, right? I mean…I came to ask for your help."

The man behind Turner walked past him into the room and took a seat beside the woman. "Nothing wrong with being curious," he said in a friendly and jovial tone. "We have nothing to hide. We are scientists. I'm a geologist, Mirna studies ancient civilizations, and Yules is a mathematician. The Spiders hired us to do a job. Nothing mysterious about that."

He didn't explain the habitat, but Turner thought it smarter not to push for an answer.

Mirna stared at him. Her eyes were the color of jade. He also noted the pale shade of her skin. "How do you know that Spiders built the habitat?" she asked.

"I've been watching your camp, debating if I should take a chance contacting you." He shrugged. "I didn't know if you'd be friendly."

"We are." Her teeth shone white between red lips as she gave him a little smile. "You know, you might be able to help us. You say you're a prospector and you've been here for five years?"

He nodded. "That's correct."

"Then you know this planet quite well, don't you?"

He chuckled. "As well as anyone, I guess. Nobody will ever really know Epsilon. Too much jungle, too many swamps, and too many lakes. Getting around with a vehicle is extremely difficult. That's why I usually travel on foot, with only my pack animals. Most prospectors do. It's the only way to find anything."

"What are you actually searching for?"

"Anything of value. Epsilon is rich in gemstones." He took the pack off his shoulder and reached inside. Pulling out one of the sapphires, he held it in his hand. "Plenty of these around."

Yules gave a low whistle. "You've got a fortune there, my friend."

Turner laughed. "Not on Epsilon. The Trading Commission sees to that." He gave Yules a calculating look. "It's yours if you help me."

Yules smiled and threw a glance at the other man. "What do you think, Clayton? Will that be payment enough?"

Clayton seemed to study Turner. His face bore a strange expression. "Do you have more of those?"

"A couple. Why?"

"No reason. Do you have anything else that might interest us?"

Turner lifted his shoulders. "I found these today." Taking a couple of the black crystal spheres, he handed them to Clayton. He felt suddenly cautious. These people came across as friendly and hospitable, but were they? They could rob him of his possessions and kill him. Nobody would ever know.

Clayton gave one of the spheres to the woman. She balanced it in her hand. Her jade-colored eyes were still on Turner. There was something about her that he couldn't put his finger on, something mysterious, cold. He held her gaze for a moment before he turned his attention to Clayton. "Like I said, you can have the gemstone if you let me stay here with you until my people pick me up. You must have a communicator I could use. Mine isn't powerful enough."

"You can stay with us," Clayton said, "but I'm afraid we can't let you use our communicator. We don't want to advertise our presence here."

"I understand." Turner smiled faintly. "Again, it is not my business to pry into yours."

"No, it isn't," Mirna said. "We'll give you shelter as long as you don't ask too many questions. You may even keep your precious beautiful rock. We have no need of it. You can do one thing though and tell us where you found these black crystals."

"I can to that. What is it about them that pique your interest?"

She smiled. "Remember what I said…no questions."

"All right. I'll show you."

"Good. Tomorrow morning." She turned her head to look at Clayton. "Maybe our new friend can speed up our search."

Clayton nodded. "It seems so. I only hope our readings are correct."

"They are," she assured him. "My…our…employers have more powerful instruments than yours."

"I've been going over these figures and it seems we are right on top of our target. All we need to do is find a way in." Yules said, taking his eyes off his small computer screen.

"We will, with the help of our guest." Mirna smiled at Turner. "By the way, what is your name?"

"Gilbert Turner," he said, staring into her glittering eyes. "I've never seen a woman with eyes like yours," he said. "Where are you from?"

"No questions. Are you forgetting?"

"No but I'm still curious." Turner looked at Yules. "You gave me the Belter-sign. I assume you are a Belter?"

Yules shrugged. "No reason to keep it a secret. Yes, I am. Born and raised in the wormholes of an asteroid circling the sun between Mars and Jupiter. I suppose you are one of us?"

Turner nodded. "I was born on Dawson."

"I know of it. The first asteroid to get artificial habitats. You can actually live on large areas of its surface." He sighed. "My community was not rich enough to do that. I spent the first ten years of my life roaming the tunnels of a piece of rock less than five miles in diameter. It was so small it didn't even have a name, only a number. I was nearly eleven when my father took me up to the surface for the first time in a spacesuit much too large for my size. That was also the first time I saw a spaceship."

"Must have been exciting." Turner remembered the first time he was allowed on a spaceship. He was five. His father took him into the mining zone of the Belt. Against his mother's wishes.

"It scared the hell out of me." Yules chuckled. "Still does, sometimes."

"And you?" Turner looked at Clayton. "Are you a Belter also?"

"Sure am." Clayton nodded. "Ceres is my birthplace."

"Ceres, the largest asteroid in the Asteroid Belt. You have habitats."

"Yes, we do. I grew up on Ceres, but I've spent some time on Earth. Didn't really like it there. Too many people, and the sky is too high."

Yules put away his computer. "Would you like a drink?"

"Wouldn't mind. I am thirsty." He grimaced. "And hungry."

"We can offer you a beer and a steak. Our ship's computer is quite sophisticated when it comes to making food. Mind you, the steak isn't the real thing, but you can hardly tell the difference. Maybe tomorrow we can go hunting for some real meat. I hear dinosaur steaks taste pretty good."

Turner laughed. "Everything tastes good when you're hungry. Besides, you can get used to about anything. There is no shortage of things to eat on Epsilon, neither is there a shortage of things that want to eat you."

Clayton, who had been listening with interest, said, "That's why I can't understand the attraction this planet seems to possess. How can you even survive by yourself in such a hostile environment?"

"By being on guard at all times. By keeping your eyes and ears open." Turner smiled grimly. "And by spotting the beast that hunts you before it has a chance to pounce on you and by being fast and accurate with your rifle."

"And you are all that?" Mirna asked.

"I've survived for five years. I guess I am all that," Turner said.

She smiled, her strange eyes shimmering. "Then perhaps it was a lucky strike you came to our camp. We can use a man like you, Turner."

"I'll go get the food." Yules left through a door in the back.

"Take the weight off your feet," Clayton said.

Turner accepted his invitation and sank into the offered seat. A feeling of exhaustion suddenly threatened to overcome him. Grimacing, he said, "I guess fighting the jungle all day is finally taking its toll."

"Speaking of fighting, I don't see any weapon that could stand up against those ferocious carnosaurs," Clayton said.

"I left my flash rifle up in the rocks. Didn't want to take the chance I might come across as a hostile intruder and get shot at."

"That was probably a smart idea." Mirna looked at his hip. "I see you didn't leave your sidearm behind."

Turner touched the butt of his gun. "A little insurance never hurts. I didn't know how I would be greeted."

"I suggest you get your rifle in the morning." Mirna smiled. "Now that we know you're not a hostile intruder. That rifle might come in handy should we face some real danger."

"If you're talking about those giant reptiles inhabiting the jungle, I agree it is a great asset to have, but from what I observed you have your own weapons capable of dealing with those critters."

Her face stayed expressionless, but he didn't miss the momentarily narrowing of her eyes. "What do you mean?"

He shrugged. Keeping his voice neutral, he said, "I saw those Spiders slicing one of the carnosaurs in half. That's quite some weapon."

She stayed silent for a moment. Then she said, "The Spiders, they do have superior weapons. Humans would be wise to realize that."

"As far as I know we have no quarrel with the Spider race." Turner gave her an inquiring look. "Has something happened while I'm stuck here looking for gems?"

"Nothing has happened," Clayton said, throwing a glance in Mirna's direction. "She likes to say things like that. Believes it makes her mysterious."

"Doesn't it?" Mirna stared at Turner. "There is something you might want to know about me."

He returned her stare, wondering what she was about to reveal. "There is much I'd like to know about you," he said with a low voice.

"I'm not human." When she smiled, she displayed needle-thin fangs. He had not noticed them before.

"I had my suspicions," he said. "What are you?"

"I don't know. A group of miners found me floating in space."

"Floating in space?"

She chuckled. "Inside a spacesuit. I have no memory how I got there. In fact, I have no memory of my life before that."

Turner looked at Clayton. "Is she messing with my mind?"

"No, she's telling you the truth. We've talked to the miners who found her. Mirna never lies, that's one thing about her. When she decides to tell you something you can be sure it is true. I question the wisdom of her decision to tell a stranger the truth, but then again…" He shrugged, "She's Mirna. And she's not human. I don't know how her brain works."

Yules walked in and carried a couple of plastic plates filled with steaming food. He handed one to Clayton and one to Turner. "Steak and boiled tubers."

Turner accepted the plate, noticed a fork and a knife beside the piece of broiled meat. "Thanks. What about that beer?"

"Coming up." Yules left again and came back a moment later with another plate and three plastic bottles. He gave one bottle to Turner.

Turner began eating. The meat tasted good. When he looked up, he saw Mirna watching him. He didn't see food in front of her. "You're not eating?" he asked.

She shook her head, still staring at him. "My body requires different nourishment. I don't eat meat."

"What do you eat?"

Her teeth flashed in a wide smile. Again, he noticed the long incisors. "My system cannot process solid food. I take it in liquid form. I prefer it warm and directly from its source."

Turner suddenly understood. The color of her skin should have given him a clue. "You're a vampire. You drink blood."

She nodded. "Don't worry, I'm not going to attack you in your sleep and suck your veins dry. I choose my donors with care and I don't only take. I give in return."

He didn't need to ask, he could guess. He had heard of creatures like her. But he asked anyway. "What do you give?"

"Pleasure. Incredible sexual pleasure you've most likely never experienced before. Ask Clayton or Yules."

Clayton chuckled. "Again, she's telling the truth." He took a swig from his bottle. "I believe she's chosen you as her donor tonight. Maybe you should eat another steak. You have a wonderful but strenuous night ahead of you."

Mirna chuckled and said, "Don't bother with another steak. I can't wait that long."

Swallowing his last bite, Turner watched Mirna walking toward him. Her eyes were wide open and seemed to glow with an intense fire; her teeth gleamed white between her open lips. Standing in front of him, she opened the front of her shirt, exposing her breasts, but he barely looked at them. His eyes were locked with hers. A strange pulling inside his head scrambled his thoughts and he became aware of a sudden pounding in his loins.

He wanted her badly and he knew he would give her whatever she asked of him. Oblivious of his surroundings and the other two men, he reached out and clawed at her skintight pants in an effort to push them past her hips.

"Don't be too eager," she whispered, the long, needle-thin incisors gleaming brightly in her open mouth as they hovered inches away from his throat. "We have all night…"

* * * *

The surface of the habitat the Spiders built seemed to swallow the light streaming down from the Primary. Turner studied it with interest.

"Quite a marvel of engineering, isn't it?" Yules said.

"It certainly is. I've never seen one erected this fast," Turner commented. "Those Spiders have a better method than our construction robots." He looked at Yules. "I know I'm not supposed to ask questions, but I'm curious. I've noticed the ones who actually built this were larger and of a different color. Are there two different species of Spiders?"

"The construction crew consists of robots, the same as our crews. Except these ones were built in the image of their creators…the Spiders." Yules smiled. "You see, in many ways the Spiders are really not much different from us."

"I wouldn't know," Turner said. "I've never had dealings with them."

"You'd be surprised to know some colonists at the fringes of controlled Human Space trade with the Spiders." Yules seemed to be in a chatty mood.

"You are right, that does surprise me," Turner said. "It is well known the Spiders don't want anything from us." He threw a glance at the large Spider ship sitting silently beside the habitat. "Where are those Spider robots hiding?"

"They're not hiding. They are still busy inside the habitat," Yules said.

"They certainly are quiet workers."

Yules chuckled. "Yes, they are but quite efficient." His eyes rested on Turner's face. "Now that you've been initiated by Mirna, we consider you one of us. Do you remember anything about last night?"

Turner wiped his hand across his forehead, trying hard to remember…*Her naked body moved slowly above him. Her breasts pressed against his chest, soft and warm. Hot lips touched his neck. A moment of sharp pain…then pleasure…great pleasure…*

The memory faded as he thought about it. Only flashes remained…*Naked breasts swung in front of his face like two pale*

*pendulums...strong thighs pressed against his hips...Eyes glowed in the
dark. White fangs slashed...pierced...*

He put his hand against his throat; felt the throbbing of his artery.

"Are you all right?"

Turner shook his head to clear it. "I'm fine," he murmured. "I can't
seem to remember much."

Yules smiled. "That is normal. Next time you'll be more aware and
you'll enjoy it much more. She's quite a woman."

"I thought she wasn't human."

"She isn't, but she's a female with great passion. Human on the
outside. Inside?" He shrugged and spread his hands.

As if on cue, Mirna appeared in the doorway of the shuttle. She
jumped out, landed on the soft ground with a graceful bending of her
knees. She was dressed in a skintight outfit that accentuated her curvy
body. Her blond hair hung loosely around her shoulders.

"It's a beautiful day," she announced. She walked up to Turner and
gave him a wide smile. "You look so much better with that beard gone
from your face."

"I feel better," he said. "Clayton assured me this morning that the
cream he gave me will keep my beard from growing for at least a year."

"I like my men to be clean-shaven." She ran a finger down his neck.
Her white incisors gleamed in the bright sunlight. "I enjoyed last night,"
she whispered. "It was obvious you haven't been with a woman for a
long time."

"I haven't," he said slowly, looking up at her and into her jade-
colored eyes. It wasn't a lie. The queen of the Eer couldn't be considered
a woman, female but not a woman in the human sense. "Question
is...was I with a woman last night?"

"I believe you know the answer to that. Did I not satisfy you?" Her
laughter mocked him.

"I remember very little about last night," he said. "How about you?
Are you satisfied?"

She bent to put her lips against his ear and teased him with her
tongue. Then she whispered, "I am extremely satisfied. It was refreshing
to drink new blood." She chuckled into his ear. "I have to admit, you are
well endowed. That was a pleasant extra bonus."

"Well, I'm happy for you," he murmured, embarrassed by her intimate behavior. He saw Yules watching, but the other man didn't say anything.

Mirna pulled away, stretched her tall, lithe body and yawned, reminding Turner of a ferocious jungle beast. "Where is Clayton?" she asked.

"He went hunting," Yules said. "He's determined to get some dinosaur steaks."

"I hope he knows what he's doing," Turner commented. "The hunter may easily become the hunted."

Yules laughed. "Don't you worry about Clayton. He can take care of himself. He spent two years prospecting on Devil's Nest. Most of the wildlife there is avian. You'd never think birds could grow that huge and still fly. Oh yes, he knows how to survive in a harsh environment."

"Every planet is different," Turner said. "There are others dangers aside from large dinosaurs on Epsilon." He slapped at an insect that tried to settle on his face. "Some are so devious and unobtrusive you don't notice them until it's too late." He adjusted the range of his insect repeller. Looking at Yules, he said, "Since I'm one of you now, how about letting me have a peek inside that habitat?"

"Who said you are one of us?" Mirna asked.

"Yules did. Apparently, being screwed by you initiated me into your clan."

"I wasn't aware we were a clan." She gave Yules a penetrating stare.

"His words, not mine," Yules said defensively.

She shrugged. "I guess it'll be all right." She smiled mysteriously. "You won't be going anywhere in the near future, since you're under my control now."

Turner looked at her sharply. "What do you mean?"

"She means she injected a substance into you, which lets her take over the motor functions of your body if she feels like it," Yules said. "That is part of the deal. The price you pay for the pleasure she bestows on you." With a little grin he added, "She'll find you wherever you are. You can't hide from her."

"I don't believe you." Turner stared at Mirna.

She smiled and nodded. "It's true." Her eyes seemed to glow with a sudden silvery fire.

He felt a strange sensation inside his head and became aware of a pulsing in his loins. He wanted her badly. His desire for her was so strong, he began walking toward her, determined to rip the clothing from her body, throw her to the ground, plunge his manhood into her…

The desire was gone as quickly as it came over him. He stood, put his hands against his pounding temples and looked at her with anger when she laughed.

"You are one of us now," she said. "Come, I will show you the inside of the habitat."

He followed her, his mind in turmoil, trying to digest what just took place. How could she make him feel that way? What had she done to him?

She stopped and chuckled, waiting for him to catch up with her. "Cheer up, next time you will be fully aware of our joining and will experience pleasures beyond your imagination. That's a promise. Yules and Clayton will testify to that."

"You raped me," he said, angrily.

"I did what I had to do to ensure my survival," she said. "I'm giving more than I receive. It is a good trade, you'll see."

"I don't like to do anything I'm forced to do," he said, stubbornly.

"When the desire comes over you, you will want to join with me." She laughed. "Even before our joining, you wanted me. I saw it in your eyes. You were not difficult to persuade."

"That was different. My emotions were my own."

"That's what you believe. That's what every male believes when he inhales the pheromones a female exudes or when his eyes undress a beautiful woman. There is no difference." She walked on, swinging her hips enticingly.

His eyes took in the lines of her voluptuous body, riveted on her full buttocks. The urge to put his hands on them and squeeze them was strong.

She looked back over her shoulder. "Now do you understand what I mean? I did nothing to your mind. You did that yourself."

"Are you reading my mind?" he asked.

"No, but I knew exactly what you were thinking and how you would react to my body. Now, come on. Don't sulk. You are about to see something not many Humans have been allowed to see."

He walked on, reluctantly, but also eager to see the inside of the alien habitat.

A door irised open as they approached. Mirna stepped through and Turner followed her into the semidarkness. After his eyes adjusted, he let out a sound of surprise. There was nothing there that even remotely resembled the inside of a habitat built by Humans.

Round mounds covered the ground. Dark openings suggested tunnels. The gray Spider robots were moving swiftly above the mounds, spinning webs that reached up to the roof of the habitat. Large spheres with openings leading into their interior hung suspended at regular intervals between the ground and the roof.

Turner noticed he could not see the sky, unlike when inside a dome built and inhabited by Humans. "They are getting ready for the Spiders to move in," he said, as the truth dawned on him.

Mirna stood in front of him, watching his reaction. "Did you think they were building this for Humans?" she asked.

"I didn't know what to think," he admitted. "The Solar Union will never allow this."

She laughed softly. "The Spiders won't ask the Solar Union, because Epsilon will soon belong to them." She pulled on his arm. "Time to leave. You've seen enough."

Turner squinted for a moment against the bright light when he stepped outside again. He stared at the closing opening. "Now what?" he asked.

"Normally I would have to kill you now," Mirna said. "But as I said before, you are here to stay. You won't tell anyone. There is no need to kill you." She chuckled. "It would be a shame to deprive me of a good source of nourishment and pleasure." She looked toward the swamp. "There is Clayton. Let's see if he had a successful hunt."

Clayton walked slowly, dragging a long body behind him. When he came closer, Turner saw that it was a small lizard. One of the plant eaters.

"It seems you are a great hunter after all," Mirna greeted him.

Clayton grinned. "We shall eat dinosaur steaks tonight."

"You took quite a chance dragging that thing," Turner said. "You could have attracted the attention of a number of meat eaters. The large kind."

"Oh, I did. One of the big boys challenged me but…" He patted his flash rifle. "This baby took care of him. Now he's fodder for his larger friends. Reminds me of Devil's Nest, like the time when I was attacked by a…"

"I believe I've heard that story too many times already," Yules cut him off. "Now isn't the time to tell it again."

"But Turner hasn't heard it," Clayton protested.

"Yules is right," Mirna said. "Now is not the time. We have other things to do."

"Like what?"

"I'm anxious for Turner to take us to the place where he found those items he showed us."

"All right, but let me slice off a few steaks first."

"Go ahead," Mirna said. "Don't leave the rest of that carcass lying around here. I don't want every carnosaur in the area paying us a visit. We have better things to do than wasting our energy and time on killing a bunch of hungry lizards."

Turner remembered the beast he had seen the Spiders cut in half and wondered what they had done with it. "Do the Spiders eat meat," he asked on an impulse.

Mirna laughed. "They can devour their own weight in less than a day. They are ravenous meat eaters."

"I can vouch for that. You should have seen them crawling all over the carnosaur they brought down a few days ago. They had a feast," Yules said.

"They ate it raw?" Turner asked.

"Hide and everything," Clayton said, chuckling.

"That's barbaric." Turner shook himself as he imagined a dozen hungry mandible-clicking hairy Spiders tearing out chunks of dinosaur meat, spattering blood and intestines all over themselves.

"From our perspective I guess it is," Yules agreed. "But remember, they are not human. You can't compare their ways of living with ours. I know of quite a few reptilian races that eat only raw meat."

"I also am aware of them." After glancing at Mirna, Turner said, "You are right. We can't always assume members of another species act like Humans… I know of someone who drinks fresh blood. I find that repugnant."

"It is no more repugnant than cutting apart the body of a creature, roasting it over a fire and then eating it." Mirna sounded amused.

"Do the Spiders eat Humans?"

Yules shrugged. "I can't answer that because I don't know."

Turner looked at Mirna. "How about you."

"I've never seen them eat Humans, but that doesn't mean they don't," she said.

"It wouldn't surprise me if they did." Turner watched Clayton slice off a large chunk of meat from the lizard's back. It was obvious Clayton did have some idea of an animal's anatomy and he knew the best cuts of meat.

Clayton stood up and held the bloody piece of meat in his hand. He grinned proudly. "This will taste great," he said. "Better than that artificial stuff we've been eating. I'll roast it on a real fire tonight."

"Put it into the refrigeration unit and let's get moving," Mirna said.

Turner had been mulling over something Mirna said before. "You told me you don't remember your life before those miners found you. How long ago was that?"

"Three years…at least," she told him. "Why is that so important?"

"You seem to have an extensive knowledge about the Spiders. How did you come into such knowledge?"

She shrugged. "The miners I lived with traded with the Spiders. One day the Spiders asked me if I was interested in a job and I accepted."

"How about Yules and Clayton?" He threw a look at Yules. "How do you fit into the picture?"

"Mirna hired us. She found us in a bar." He grinned. "You'd be surprised how many deals are made in bars. Some of them turn out, some don't. I hope this one turns out."

"It will," Mirna assured him. Her eyes fell on Turner. "How far is it to the place where you found those crystals?"

"About ten miles in a straight line. We can make it there in less than four hours. There are a couple of swamps we have to skirt. And it depends on how many meat eaters we have to hide from."

Mirna looked at the sun. "About six hours of traveling time. I'd suggest we don't dawdle any longer and get going."

* * * *

They were on their way thirty minutes later. Turner retrieved his flash rifle, glad to feel the cool metal and the comforting weight in his hands. He took the lead, following his navigator. Mirna walked behind him, then Yules, with Clayton guarding their rear.

"I notice you are well equipped to navigate in this jungle," Mirna remarked.

Turner chuckled. "If it weren't for this little gadget I'd be lost in a short time. The route I took finding your camp is in the navigator's memory. As long as I don't stray too far from the original trail I'm okay. You can't rely on a compass because of the magnetic interference. For some reason there seems to be a lot of it in this area."

"Did you hear that, Yules?" Mirna called to the man behind her.

"Hear what?"

"Turner says there is a lot of magnetic interference in the area. That's a good sign, isn't it?"

"I would think so." Yules sounded cautious. "It could mean anything. I wouldn't hold my breath...not yet anyway."

Turner stopped and held up a hand. The sudden silence in the jungle confirmed his suspicion.

"What is it?" Mirna asked.

Turner put a finger against his lips. "Something big," he mouthed.

They stood near an Octopus Tree. Its thick root system would give them protection should the need arise.

Clayton was the first one to spot the giant head of the Rex as it pushed its way into the clearing ahead of them. "Over there," he whispered.

The beast had come silently and would have surprised them in the open had it not been for Turner's uncanny ability to detect and recognize a threat. It had saved his life many times in the past.

These behemoths could move through the thick ferns and mushroom trees with great stealth when they were stalking prey, but they could also move with lightening speed, much faster than a predator of their size should be able to.

The long dagger-teeth gleamed with a dull sheen between the powerful open jaws as the carnosaur surveyed the clearing.

Turner looked into the small eyes that seemed fixed on the four pitiful small Humans and he knew the Rex was aware of them. Had been aware of them long before it made its appearance. "Hide!" he shouted. Without waiting for his companions, he sprinted for the Octopus Tree and threw himself flat onto the ground. Crawling as fast he could manage into the tangle of the massive root system, he could hear the others doing the same.

A terrifying roar made him hug the ground. He felt the thud vibrating through the roots as the giant lizard hit the trunk of the tree. Even though he knew he was safe, he couldn't still the sudden thumping of his heart.

"That was close," a voice said nearby.

He turned his head to see Clayton lying behind a thick root on his right. "Is everyone safe?" he asked.

"I think so," Clayton said, his breath coming out in gasps.

"I'm here," Yules called from the other side.

"Where is Mirna?"

"I don't know."

Chapter Four

It was dark inside the mass of gnarled roots. Turned searched the darkness for a sign of the woman.

"Mirna?" Clayton called. When there was no answer, he cursed, "Dammit!"

"She was right behind me," Yules said.

They stopped talking when the carnosaur roared again. Turner could see the bulk of the beast through the entwined roots. The Rex was visibly enraged and it smashed its thick tail into the roots of the Octopus Tree over and over, trying to get at the quarry hiding inside them.

"I hope this tree doesn't collapse on top of us," Clayton said.

"Don't worry, we're quite safe. This is not the first time I used this type of tree to hide from predators," Turner assured him.

"I dropped my rifle before I crawled in here," Yules said. "I feel helpless without it."

"I wonder what happened to Mirna." Clayton sounded worried.

The Rex bellowed again. Then the dark shadow of its body seemed to move away. Yules began crawling toward the border of the root system. "Maybe I can get my rifle," he said.

"Be careful," Turner warned. "These beasts are cunning. It may be waiting for us to leave this protection. The moment you do it will pounce on you."

Yules reached the edge of the roots. "I can't see it. Maybe it is gone," he called back. Then he cursed. "Dammit! That son of a bitch stepped on my rifle and broke it."

Turned wormed his way toward the small opening. He froze when a loud roar erupted from nearby and ended abruptly. The ground shook beneath him as something fell with a crashing sound. Something huge and heavy.

Watching from his hiding place, Turner listened, hearing nothing but the erratic dull sound of something pounding the ground in the otherwise absolute silence. Then he heard soft footsteps approaching. A slim shadow blocked the entrance to his hiding place.

"You can come out now. It is safe," said a woman's voice.

"Mirna?" Clayton called, chuckling. "I should have known better than to worry about your safety."

Turner crawled out from under the roots and brushed off his clothing. The soil underneath the tree was moist and sticky from an oily substance the roots released into the ground.

The bulky body of the Rex lay not far away. The scaly tail was twitching, thrashing the vegetation near it, but Turner knew the beast was dead.

He looked at Mirna, who watched him with a bemused expression. She still held her energy rifle in both hands, as if ready to shoot something else. "They may be big, but they can be killed," she said.

"How did you manage to escape?" he asked.

"I climbed a tree," she said, smiling.

"Nobody can climb a tree that fast." Turner shook his head in disbelief.

"Mirna can," Yules said behind him. "She can do a lot of things ordinary Humans can't." He held his bent rifle in his hands. Now he turned it around and studied it.

"Can she fix your rifle?" Turner asked.

Yules grimaced. "I'm afraid this one is beyond fixing." Opening the power supply compartment, he removed the energy rods and shoved them into his pocket. He gave the twisted weapon one last look and then he threw it into the thick ferns. He patted his sidearm. "Lucky I still have this. It may not be as powerful as the rifle but still better than a slingshot." He grinned. "I've never used a slingshot but that is the only comparison I could come up with."

"I have," Clayton said. "On *Angel's Nest*. The natives there have perfected them. They fill the nut-like fruit of a tree with explosives. You wouldn't believe the damage they can inflict. So don't knock slingshots, my friend."

Turner walked up to the carnosaur and circled the giant beast. He found the severed head not far away from the body. The eyes were open and staring as if they were still alive. The gaping jaws displayed long teeth. He looked at the stump of the neck, noticing the cauterized wound.

The results of using an energy weapon were always the same. The searing heat of the blast coagulated the sliced tissue, preventing the carcass from bleeding out.

He found that Mirna had followed him and turned to give her a sour look. "There is plenty of blood here for you to indulge yourself," he said. "And it is fresh."

She chuckled, refusing to take his bait. "I'm still satisfied from last night," she said.

"How can that sustain you for so long? I'm ready to stop and eat something. Don't you get de-hydrated?"

"Of course I do. When I get thirsty I suck on some vegetable or fruit."

"I thought you only drank blood?"

"I said I don't eat meat, but I never said I don't drink liquids." She laughed. "There is much you don't know about me." She prodded the scaly neck with her booted foot. "This is a lot of meat. Why don't *you* eat some of it?"

"I'm not that desperate for food. It would require too much work to get at the tender parts. There are other, better sources." When a shrill scream erupted behind him he swung around, brought up his flash rifle. He recognized the sound and the new danger. Before he could push the firing stud of his weapon, he heard the discharge of Mirna's rifle and saw the body of the Raptor, which had appeared in the clearing, fall to the ground. Another one came out of the thicket and Turner fired his rifle into the open beak-like maw.

Clayton and Yules fired at the same time he did. He hadn't seen their targets, but he heard bodies fall.

Four down, he thought but didn't relax. He knew the Raptors traveled in large packs. Holding his rifle ready to be fired, he scanned the nearby ferns for movement.

Raptors were smart and cunning. The four they had killed were the smaller ones, the young ones; none of them larger than eight feet from head to tail. The older ones hung back as the young Raptors rushed in, hoping to find their prey engaged with the young ones when they made their appearance.

The first of the adults exploded into the open with a roaring scream, tail curled up, narrow, long jaws wide open.

This time Turner was the first to shoot. The released energy from his flash rifle burned a huge hole into the Raptor's scaly but soft chest. The momentum of its rush carried it toward the four people, but then it went down, jaws still snapping.

Mirna sliced the second one neatly in half before it even stepped fully out of the ferns.

I'll have to get one of those rifles, Turner thought fleetingly as he burned a hole into the third Raptor that had been close behind the second. He heard a loud scream of rage coming from his right and saw another of the beasts rushing out of the thick ferns. Before he could swing his rifle around, one of the other two men brought the beast down, but not before it almost reached Turner and Mirna. It crashed to the ground only a couple of feet away from them, razor-sharp claws almost touching Mirna's booted legs.

"That was too damn close!" Turner cursed. He kept a watchful eye on the ferns and high grass, but the last of the Raptors seemed to have made its appearance. "We'd better leave this area as quickly as we can. All these dead carcasses will begin to decay in a short time and every scavenger in the neighborhood will smell the blood once one of them starts ripping apart the bodies."

"I agree," Clayton said. "This reminds me of the incident on…."

"Never mind that now," Yules interrupted him. "I've heard that one too many times already. I suggest we follow Turner's advice." He looked at Turner. "Which way?"

Turner checked his navigator. Then he pointed. "That way." He adjusted his pack and, after one last look at the massive bulk of the Rex, he began walking without waiting for the others. He knew they were close behind him.

After walking for about half an hour, they stopped to rest and eat something.

"Is there anything you can recommend for me?" Mirna asked.

Turner rose from his squatting position and walked over to a small bush, which he had spotted as he walked past it, and sliced off an oval-shaped furry object with his hunting knife. He cut out a hole in the top of what obviously was the fruit of the bush. Handing it to Mirna, he said,

"Here, drink this. It will quench your thirst." He smirked. "It may not fulfill your sexual craving, but it will provide you with nourishment."

She took it and smelled it. Then her jade-colored eyes locked with his. "The sexual aspect is mainly for the benefit of my donor," she said.

"Are you telling me you don't enjoy the sex when you drink blood?"

"That's not what I said. Of course, I enjoy the sex. If I didn't, I would just rip open your artery and feed until I'm sated. I'm saying when I join with a male he receives adequate payment for what I take. More than adequate, as you will find out the next time." Her lips pulled into a smile. "For now I shall be satisfied with this." She put her lips to the fruit and sucked on it.

Turner watched her, disappointed she didn't flinch when she drank the foul smelling liquid.

After a while she threw the fruit away. "I've tasted better," she commented. "But it served its purpose."

It took nearly another hour to reach the spot where Turner lost his pack animal. There was no evidence anything ever happened there. The few bits the carnosaur left where gone. Scavengers were not scarce in this jungle, and scraps of skin or bones didn't last long.

Turner skirted the deep hole under the ruined Spider-beetle net and headed for the gap in the cliffs. "I found those crystal spheres inside this cave," he explained to his companions before he squeezed through the narrow opening.

Once the others joined him, he let the beam of his torchlight play across the rubble on the floor. "Right here," he said.

Clayton shone his light at the tunnel opening leading into the interior of the mountain. "I believe we have found a way to get underground," he said, excitement coloring his words.

"Then let's enter," Mirna said.

Even thought her voice sounded as cool and composed as usual, Turner detected the same excitement he had heard in Clayton's voice and wondered what they expected to find.

Clayton, who was the geologist, took the lead as they entered the narrow tunnel that led away from the small cave in the cliff. He played the beam of his torchlight across the floor, which was littered with ragged rocks, some of them large enough to present a dangerous obstacle.

Turner was close behind him, his mind curious as to what his three new companions were searching for.

The tunnel widened after they had taken less than fifty steps and the ground began to take a gradual decline, leading the four travelers deeper underground.

"I'm surprised how cool it is," Mirna remarked from the rear.

"It certainly is a pleasant change," Yules said. "Reminds me of the asteroid where I grew up."

"Actually, this tunnel is much like the one I was in when I was captured by the fierce warriors of the *Moles* on…" Clayton started but Yules cut him off.

"Save it for another time, Clayton. Concentrate on the task at hand. I can't walk and listen to your stories of past glory-days right now. I almost tripped over one of those big rocks back there." He let out a string of loud curses. "Dammit! That one nearly broke my toes!"

Mirna laughed softly. "Perhaps they are too long and your feet too big."

"That is the nicest thing you've said to me in a long time," Yules grunted.

"Anyone mind telling me what exactly you are hoping to find down here?" Turner asked.

"Your question will be answered when we find it," Mirna said. "Until then curb your curiosity."

"I understood I was part of the clan now," Turner said.

"Only when it comes to screwing Mirna." Yules chuckled.

Clayton stopped and held up an arm.

Yules cursed when he bumped into Turner who stopped at the same time as Clayton. Clayton reached for his flash rifle, which he had slung across his back.

"What is it?" Yules asked behind him.

"Don't you hear it?" Clayton aimed his torchlight into the shadowy world ahead of them, but they didn't see anything.

"Hear what?" Yules stood listening beside Turner. It was eerily silent in the tunnel now. Not even the noise from the jungle outside penetrated the dense rock.

"Whatever it was, it's gone now," Clayton stared into the darkness. "It sounded like a soft rustling, like something scraping along the walls."

"I can still hear it," Mirna said quietly. "It sounds big. Be prepared."

Turner strained to hear but the only thing he was aware of was a distant hissing in his ears. His nerves were working overtime and he felt a slight tingling in his neck, a sure sign of looming danger. He clipped his torchlight into his belt and gripped his flash rifle with fingers suddenly damp and itchy. The light from his headlamp showed nothing but darkness.

Mirna pushed him aside as she moved forward. The blinding glare of her discharging weapon illuminated a large, shadowy body crouching in the darkness.

Bright spots floated in Turner's vision in the aftermath of the flash. He couldn't see anything, but he heard the dull thudding sounds as something heavy and large thrashed against the walls of the tunnel, followed by a low, growling bellow.

"That was close," Mirna said. "Much too close. We have to be on guard at all times from now on."

"Let's see what you bagged," Clayton said.

"I didn't bag anything. We are not hunting." Mirna's voice sounded annoyed. "No more unnecessary talking. Be careful. It may still be alive."

They walked on, their rifles ready. They didn't see anything until they came to a sharp dip in the rocky floor. In the shallow depression behind the dip lay a long grey shape. It wasn't moving, but Turner was wary.

His suspicion was correct. Clayton, who was the first to reach the unmoving creature, nearly became its victim.

With a loud hissing roar the grotesque head lifted, jaws wide open, and slashed sideways. The only thing that saved Clayton from being disemboweled was the fact that he had also been aware of the danger. He jumped back in time to avoid being sliced open by the short horn growing from the bony head.

Turner fired his rifle, aiming the ray of sizzling heat at the yawning maw. Yules opened fire simultaneously with his flash gun and sliced off a large chunk of dark flesh. Cursing, Clayton put a burst of searing light into the convulsing body.

Finally the animal lay still.

"I believe it is dead now," Yules said, his voice sounding harsh, excited. He approached the motionless carcass carefully and prodded it with his foot.

Turner relaxed and lowered his rifle. He felt his heart beating in his chest, became aware of heat rushing across his neck. The thrill of overcoming sudden danger always did that to him. Many times in the past he had asked himself why he spent his time in the jungle, facing ferocious beasts and countless other dangers. He knew the answer, even though he denied it.

He loved the rush of adrenalin, the pumping of blood through his veins and the weakness in his knees after it was over. It was like an addiction to a drug. Something he couldn't seem to live without.

"It has no eyes," Yules said into the sudden silence.

"It doesn't need them. Not here in this complete darkness," Mirna said. "Its other senses are most likely highly developed, its sense of hearing for instance. It probably detects its quarry through vibrations. Look at those tiny tendrils where the eyes should be."

"Amazing," Clayton said. "This reminds me very much of the time on *Dead Rock*…"

"Not now, Clayton," Mirna said. "Be on the alert. Let's move one."

* * * *

The tunnel widened and ended in a grotto with glistening stalactites erupting from the jagged ceiling. Turner expected to see stalagmites growing out of the ground, but he noticed only small rounded cones. He bent down to examine one and found tiny ridges running across the otherwise smooth surface.

Clayton seemed to wonder about the same thing, because he shone his light on another of the short stalagmites. "Looks like teeth marks," he commented.

"I'm thinking the same," Turner agreed. "Something is eating this stuff. Probably for the minerals."

"That means there are critters down here." Yules played the powerful beam of his torchlight across the grotto.

"Small ones," Turner said.

"They could still be dangerous. Besides, small ones are eaten by bigger ones." Mirna scanned the dark shadows ahead. "Can you take a reading, Yules? We don't want to get lost down here."

Yules set down his pack and rummaged around in it. He rose and stuck something against one of the stalactites. It glowed with a green fire. "This will be our first marker." He shone his light back toward the entrance of the tunnel they had emerged from. "I'll put one over there."

He walked back to the tunnel and put another glow button against the wall. A red one.

"Looks like you came prepared," Turner said.

Yules smiled. "I've never been a friend of dark places. It's so easy to get lost in the dark. We'll be able to locate this beacon from wherever we're headed."

"Let's hope so," Turner said skeptically. "There are many radioactive and magnetic metals and crystals in these rocks playing havoc with electronic direction finders. I wouldn't count too much on your beacons."

"We can always find them by sight." Yules took his torchlight and searched the expanse of the grotto. There were dark, glistening walls on two sides, but only emptiness ahead. "I guess we'll head that way," he said.

They held their weapons ready as they walked on. Once, Turner nearly ran into one of the stalactites. He ducked just in time to avoid possible injury. The sharp point wouldn't pierce his helmet, but the ragged edges could inflict serious wounds to his unprotected face.

A scrabbling noise to his right made him turn his head. In the light of his headlamp he saw a number of small creatures dashing for cover.

"Those are probably the ones who left their teeth marks," Clayton said.

One of the little creatures crouched behind a rock not large enough to hide it from sight. It reminded Turner of a rat. He had seen plenty of them in the tunnels of Dawson.

"Looks like a rat," Clayton echoed his thoughts.

"You have them on Ceres?" Turner asked.

Clayton chuckled. "Wherever Humans go, rats go. They stow away on ships and they propagate faster than Humans. They are also more adaptable than Humans. I think one day they'll inherit the universe."

"This one is not a rat." Turner peered at the little creature.

"No rat," Mirna agreed. "But I believe it is a mammal."

"Impossible. There are no mammals on Epsilon." The light from the headlamp in Turner's helmet moved back and forth on the ground as he shook his head. "This planet belongs to the insects and reptiles."

"Nothing is impossible," Clayton said. "I've seen many impossible things on my travels to other planets."

"So we've heard." Mirna began walking. "Let's keep moving. We'll never find what we're looking for standing around discussing impossibilities."

"Whatever it is you're looking for," Turner commented, hoping to get a reaction and possibly a bit more information but nobody took the bait. He followed Mirna, his fingers clamped around his flash rifle, wondering what other creatures they might stumble across. If that snakelike reptile they had killed in the tunnel was an indication they needed to be on guard against other, possibly more ferocious, predators. Of course, where there was one there were usually more. Maybe that one had a mate somewhere roaming these caverns. It might make an appearance at any time.

It was damp in the cavern but surprisingly cool. Wiping the sweat from his forehead with a grimy hand he inhaled the humid, musky air, becoming aware of other, unidentifiable, odors. He didn't feel any fear, but this was unfamiliar territory. Something large and menacing might lurk behind the next corner or stalagmite, ready to ambush them.

He observed Yules lift his head and sniff the air.

"Smells strange," Yules said. "Almost…metallic." He cursed loudly when he stumbled over a pile of objects on the ground.

Mirna, who had taken the lead again, stopped and turned around. "What is your problem?"

Yules bent and examined the obstacles he had tripped over. Turner noticed the round glittering spheres among the shattered rocks the same time Yules discovered them. Yules picked one up and showed it to Mirna. "Look at this. The same crystalline eggs Turner found."

Mirna took it from him and studied it. "You're right." She looked at Clayton. "It seems you were correct in your assumption. I believe we will be successful in our search."

She pocketed the black crystal. "Lift up your big feet when you're walking, Yules. I don't want you tripping and hurting yourself. We can't afford wasting time patching you up."

Yules laughed good-humoredly. "I find you extremely sexy when you talk like that."

Turner listened to their friendly bantering with only half of his attention. He felt jittery. His neck tingled, the way it always did when danger lay nearby…waiting. When he turned his head to light up the area with his headlamp, shadows moved in the obscurity of the gloomy dark…ghostly images, magnified by his imagination. His nerves were still raw from the encounter with the beast they killed. His senses screamed danger, yet his searching eyes picked up nothing tangible.

Mirna seemed to share his mood, but not the same way he did. He observed the way she moved her head, the way the carried her rifle, the way she put one foot in front of the other. Like a hunter searching for quarry, whereas he felt like prey stalked by a predator. She was an enigma to him. It was obvious she was the one in charge. Yules and Clayton followed her orders without questioning her motives.

Either they were addicted to her sexual attention or they genuinely acknowledged her as their leader. He became more and more curious to find out about their mission on Epsilon.

A dark shadow loomed suddenly in front of them. Mirna had been on guard. Her rifle came up. A bundle of energy struck the large form. It fell with a roar that ended abruptly as the creature died.

Turner caught a glimpse of sharp teeth and snapping jaws as a second beast jumped over its fallen companion. He fired from the hip into the gaping maw, registered with satisfaction when it crashed to the ground, on top of the other one.

Beside him, Yules and Clayton fired their weapons. He didn't have time to look at their targets. His attention was diverted by something large coming at him from his left side. He swung around, fired once. The beast fell, jaws snapping, claws reaching toward him. His second shot brought down another of the creatures.

The air was filled with enraged screams and ear-deafening roars coming from many throats. The flashes from discharging rifles lit up the cavern, displaying dark shadowy forms slinking among the stalagmites.

He had no time to think as his body reacted instinctively, his finger holding down the firing stud of his rifle. The released bolts of energy burned into his attackers, piled bodies upon bodies.

Then as suddenly as it began it was over.

The cavern seemed eerily silent.

Turner became aware of his beating heart, his rapid breathing, of his sweaty hands gripping a rifle nearly too hot to touch. The sudden weakness in his knees told him they had killed the last one, but he kept his rifle up as his eyes tried to pierce the darkness for signs of more of them.

"I believe we killed them all," Clayton said into the silence.

"We might have just wiped out a whole tribe," Yules said, his breath coming out in loud, hoarse gasps. With a wild laugh, he lifted his flash gun above his head. "That was exhilarating. We are like gods. Nothing can touch us."

"We were lucky," Mirna said, damping his elation. "Look at those claws and teeth."

"Giant frogs," Clayton observed.

Turner studied the creatures they had killed. The size of a large dog, they did indeed look like giant frogs. Their wide mouths were studded with long, sharp teeth. Just like the first beast they had encountered in the tunnel, these had no eyes, only a mass of short tendrils above their nose slits.

"They are literally creatures of darkness," Clayton said. "They remind me very much of the…"

He stopped talking when Mirna interrupted him, "We know. The *Vellans* in the caverns of Wormworld. I'm quite certain these are different. Much more dangerous."

"Well, they are similar."

Turner stared at the dead bodies. "There must be at least two dozen of them."

"I think more like three." Mirna prodded one with her foot. "They look reptilian, but I believe they are half mammalian. See the row of teats on the bellies of some of them? That means they are bearing live young."

"I've been on Epsilon for over five years and I've never seen a mammalian creature," Turner said.

"Seems there is a lot more to this planet than Humans are aware of," Clayton mused. "Perhaps that is why other races are suddenly so interested in it."

"Who are these other races?" Turner asked.

"Some of the Dragons and the Spiders."

"Why would the existence of mammals be of any interest to the Reptilians or the Spiders, for that matter?"

"There might be other things here than mammals." Yules sounded mysterious.

Turner gave him a sharp look. "I'm more and more curious what it is you are hoping to find down here. It might help if someone gave me a hint."

"You'll find out soon enough," Mirna said. She threw Yules a warning look. "You talk too much."

Yules chuckled. "What is the difference if he knows now or later?"

"Let me be the judge of that!" Mirna spoke sharply. Her eyes still rested on Yules. "You have been a bit argumentative lately. I believe you and I need to join. It is time for me to feed anyway."

"Now?"

"Yes, now. Clayton and Turner can stay guard."

"I'm not really in the mood."

Mirna's demeanor was suddenly soft and seductive. Her lips curved into a smile. She touched Yules on the cheek and looked into his eyes. "This only confirms it. You never said that before. Don't worry, you'll be." She grabbed his arm and led him behind one of the stalagmites. Yules followed meekly, a sheep to be slaughtered.

Turner turned away from them, but not before he saw Mirna open the buckle of Yules's belt. He was not in the habit of watching a couple copulating. Of course, having sexual intercourse with Mirna was something completely different. She was satisfying much more than her sexual craving.

He tried to shut out the sounds, but hearing their moans and heavy breathing, he felt a gentle fluttering in his loins. Suddenly, he wanted Mirna badly. He longed to feel her naked body pressed against his, longed for the heat between her legs, her lips on his, ached for the ecstasy of the moment when her teeth pierced his artery.

When he looked at Clayton, he saw the other man staring into the darkness. As if sensing Turner's eyes on him, Clayton twisted around and looked at him. He smiled crookedly. "She is a seductress, my friend. Once you have tasted her, you will always crave her. That is the power she has over us."

"It seems so at first, but you could break free if you wanted to. She admitted that her influence over Yules has been diminishing. That is why she chose him. She needs to get him back under her control." Turner glanced in the direction where Yules and Mirna lay on the ground. He could see her naked form moving slowly on top of Yules, her face buried against his neck.

Clayton followed his gaze. "Yes, I could, but there is more here at stake than my freedom from her," he said slowly. "Much more."

Turner watched as Mirna rose. She wiped a hand across her mouth. Her eyes locked with his when she looked up. She smiled and walked toward him, moving her naked body suggestively. Standing in front of him, she put one finger against his lips. "You want me," she purred, "I can see it in your eyes, but you will have to wait your turn. It is Clayton who needs me more than you."

Turning toward Clayton, she said, "Come."

He followed her like an automaton, without a word.

Yules came back. His face bore the expression of a man still in trance. He finished dressing and stood silent for a long time.

Turner let him be. The loud moans from Clayton seemed to echo through the grotto. It didn't help the craving of his body. Mirna was wrong. He did need her badly.

"She is not evil," Yules said suddenly.

"Perhaps not," Turner said.

"She needs to feed. Fruit juice sustains her body only for so long."

"She's not human." He fought hard to tune out the sounds of ecstasy coming from the thrashing couple. Studying the dead creatures in front of him, he tried to avert his attention. "I wonder if there are more of these waiting for us," he said.

"There probably are. These and others. Possibly even more ferocious. We need to be on guard."

Turner became aware of the silence behind the stalagmite where Mirna and Clayton lay. Moments later he saw them rise and dress.

"Ready to go on?" Mirna asked after joining them. Her jade-colored eyes glowed with bright fire. She looked vibrant and happy.

None of the men spoke. They followed her like three slaves would follow their master. Turner's mind was in turmoil, his body in a state of sexual readiness.

A buck in rut.

He knew the term, knew what it meant, even though he had never seen live animals of the kind it described. Five years in the jungles of Epsilon had not given him much of an opportunity to have a relationship with a woman. There had been one nearly three years ago in Desert Hell.

Geraldine Laymon. A couple of years older than he. Her husband had died horribly after being bitten by a poisonous reptile, leaving her lonely, afraid, and vulnerable. Thinking of her brought a sad smile to his face. They spent a short time together, but when he went back into the jungle to work the plot he had found, she got tired of waiting and hooked up with another man. He thought he was in love with her, but later he realized it had only been loneliness that brought them together. Nothing unusual on Epsilon.

Was he in love with Mirna? He knew the answer to that. What he felt for Mirna was nothing but lust.

No, not lust. Dependence. She had injected something into his system that allowed her to control his emotions and his craving for her. She had put him under her spell. Him, Clayton, and Yules. All three men were eagerly waiting for her to throw them a bone.

Dogs competing for their master's favors.

Clayton's voice ripped him out of his contemplation.

"Over there...a lake."

Turner followed Clayton's pointing finger. He saw the reflection of Clayton's torchlight dancing across the dark surface of what looked like water.

"Be careful. This could be the place where those oversized frogs live," Mirna warned.

They approached the lake with care, weapons in hand. A soft splashing sound from the middle of the lake made Turner freeze, lift his rifle, but then it was silent again. When he shone his torchlight on the water, he saw a ring of ripples spreading across the surface.

"Something small," Yules said. "Nothing to worry about."

"Just because whatever caused those ripples is small, doesn't mean we can let down our guard," Mirna chided him. "Something large could be chasing it."

Moving along the shore of the underground lake, senses alert, they didn't encounter any dangers, and Turner breathed a sigh of relief when they left the water behind. He heard one more splash, a little louder than the first one, but nothing came out of the lake to pursue them.

He noticed that the stalagmites and stalactites became fewer and fewer until suddenly the cavern was without any obstructions, except for large and small boulders strewn across the ground.

Clayton sniffed the air. "Is it just my imagination or is it not as damp down here?"

"No, you're not imagining it. I've also noticed that," Yules said.

A fluttering noise above their heads made all four of them look up. Turner unclipped his torch and aimed it at the ceiling. It was covered with small, winged creatures clinging to the rugged surface. Some of them crawled along the ceiling, some just hung motionless, while a large number flew in circles around small holes in the rock.

"Bats," Turner said.

"As long as they don't want to suck my blood, I have no problem with them," Yules said.

"Be silent!" Mirna ordered in a low voice. "We don't know anything about these creatures. They are small, but they could be poisonous. They may be attracted by sound waves coming from our mouths, so be quiet."

The walls began to close in on either side; the cavern became a tunnel, barely wide enough for two people to walk abreast. Turner walked beside Mirna, his eyes straining to penetrate the darkness ahead. After a while the tunnel split in two.

"We'll take this one," Mirna decided. "We can always come back if it leads nowhere."

Yules stuck one of his beacons against the wall before they entered the tunnel. They had barely walked a hundred feet when the tunnel split again. Mirna decided to stick to the larger one.

After traveling the tunnel for about an hour it ended against a rugged wall. Two tunnels led in opposite directions.

"Let's go left," Mirna said.

Turner, who had taken the lead, spotted it first. Before he could say anything, Yules spoke up. "It seems we've walked in a circle. There is the beacon I left."

"Well, I guess it is the other tunnel we have to take. It has to lead somewhere." Mirna wasn't fazed by it. "We've lost an hour, that's all."

"I've never liked tunnels," Clayton remarked.

Turner chuckled. "That sounds strange coming from a man who was born on an asteroid."

"That's why I don't like tunnels. It reminds me too much of my childhood. I got lost once roaming the tunnels on Ceres. We may get lost down here."

"That's why the beacons. We won't get lost," Yules assured him. "I'll put a second marker beside the first one. That way we'll know if we come back here again. Besides, each beacon has a different number. I'll be able to tell on my locater where exactly we are."

They followed the narrower tunnel with trepidation; at least Turner did. He didn't know how the others felt. Mirna seemed to be unafraid, but she was not human. Her expressions and feeling were different. If she had any feelings at all.

Tunnels didn't scare Turner. In fact, he felt more secure seeing the comforting walls of solid matter on either side of him, and a ceiling that didn't reach too high. That's why he liked the jungle and the canopy of the giant mushroom umbrellas. They provided protection against attacks from the sky. He knew on Epsilon that was an illusionary feeling. In the jungle, danger lurked everywhere, even in the gills of the mushroom trees. There was no safety anywhere.

The tunnel widened and opened into a large cavern. When they played the beams of their torches across its expanse, they saw a smooth wall at the end of the cavern.

Clayton expelled a whoosh of air. "I believe we found something. That wall does not look natural."

Mirna walked briskly across the rock-littered floor. She was the first one to reach the wall. Touching it with one hand, she turned and smiled. "Metal. We weren't wrong."

Yules ran his hand over the smooth surface. "There seems to be no way to breach this barrier."

"There has to be an entrance somewhere. Those crystals we found were carried out by animals. If we search the ground, we may find more crystals, which might lead us to the entrance." Mirna scrutinized the area in front of the wall. Then she began to walk along it, her head down to let her headlamp light up the floor.

The men spread out and did the same. Clayton was the one who found a cluster of the black spheres in a small heap among other rocks. Turner examined the way the spheres lay and drew an imaginary line toward the wall.

Mirna let out a small sound of pleasure when her light lit up a hole in the rocks where the metal barrier joined the rough wall of the cavern. When she shone her light on the ground, she discovered one of the black round crystals. "My assumption was correct," she said with satisfaction.

She disappeared into the dark hole in the wall. Turner was the last one to enter.

Chapter Five

The tunnel was short. It ended in another cavern, but this one was different from the ones they had passed through so far. The walls, the ceiling, and the floor were smooth...evidence of tools having been used to create them.

Turner inhaled the cool, dry air...surprised it didn't smell stale. When he saw the rows upon rows of transparent oval containers, he held his breath. Each one was filled with black spheres; the same spheres they had found on their way here. Some of the containers had cracked open and spilled the black crystals onto the smooth floor.

Mirna stood silent, as if in a trance. She turned and looked at the three men. In the light of his headlamp Turner could see the near rapture in her face. Her eyes glinted with blue fire.

"We found it." She spoke softly, but her voice did display a strange quality. It sounded almost hollow. "Your calculations were correct, Yules."

Yules didn't seem to notice the change in her; he was concentrating on an instrument he held in his hand. "According to my calculations we should be right under our camp."

"Good." Mirna began walking toward the transparent containers. "Let's inspect the eggs."

One wall was covered with screens and machinery of unfamiliar design. Turner's eyes hurt when he looked at them for a longer time. Something reached for his brain and twisted, trying to pull him toward the distorted shapes and forms.

He forced his eyes away, stumbled and fought to regain his balance.

"Do you feel that?" Clayton whispered beside him.

"This is incredible." Yules let out a deep breath. "After all this time it is still working."

"The technology of the Ancients was awesome," Mirna said. Turner had not heard her come up behind him. "Much has been lost over the millennia. We need to reclaim that knowledge."

She still sounded so different. He turned his head and looked into her face. When her eyes locked with his, he shrank back. She smiled, but even her smile had changed. "You probably wonder what this is all about?" she asked.

He could only nod.

"There is no harm in telling you now. One hundred thousand years ago, according to your calendar, there raged a terrible war between the Spiders and one of the reptilian races. It lasted for over a hundred years. The Spiders built sanctuaries on many planets where they kept millions of eggs in suspended animation to preserve their race. This is one of those sanctuaries. What you see in those containers are Spider eggs."

"Surely after all these thousands of years they are dead," Turner said.

She shook her head. "No. They are not dead but suspended in time. We will revive them."

"Why?"

"Because they are our children. We have waited a long time for this day, and so have they."

"Your children?" Turner stared at her. "You do not belong to the Spider race!" He shouted the accusation.

"That is where you are wrong. I may not look like a Spider on the outside, but inside, I am."

"I don't understand."

"I was created to look humanoid. This body was grown artificially. Even though I look human on the outside, inside I am a Spider."

"Didn't you tell me you had no idea what you were?" Turner gaped at her and then at Clayton. "You told me she never lies. Was that a lie?"

"It was not a lie," Mirna said. "I didn't know until I saw the eggs what I really was. That knowledge was kept from me for my protection."

"Did you know?" he asked Clayton.

Clayton shook his head. "No, but I had my suspicions. She knew too many things about the Spider race, things she shouldn't have known."

"This is incredible." Turner tried to absorb the sudden revelation. "You are working for the Spiders? Why?"

"Money. After this, Yules and I will be rich beyond anything we ever dreamed of."

"You are willing to betray the human race for money?"

"We are betraying nobody. It is not a well-known fact, but many colonists are trading with the Spiders. Would you call them traitors? I don't think so. We all do what we have to do to survive. This might even help the relationship between Humans and Spiders."

"How are you going to revive these eggs? If it is at all possible."

"Remember the habitat you inspected? You must have noticed something peculiar about it. It is a nursery. We will transport the eggs to the surface and they will hatch inside the specially designed hatchery."

"And how will you transport the eggs?"

Clayton chuckled. "So many questions again. Just wait and see."

"I sent out the signal," Yules said. "They should begin with the drilling shortly."

"Good." Mirna studied the cavern. "There is nothing we can do until then. I want to explore the rest of the sanctuary." She began walking away.

Turner looked again at the twisted angles of the machines. Immediately he felt the wrenching in his mind, became aware of the beating of his heart, the beads of perspiration forming on his forehead. "There is something about this place that is completely alien," he said hoarsely. "We cannot let this fall into the Spiders' possession."

"It belongs to them," Yules said. "Don't you understand that, Turner? Their ancestors built this for the future preservation of their race. It is not ours to take."

"They will challenge our right to be on Epsilon," Turner said.

"They already have, my friend." Yules sighed. "I guess you don't know?"

"Know what?"

"That the Spiders have a battleship ready to protect what is theirs."

"Where?"

"Just beyond this Star System."

"Do they want war?"

Yules lifted his shoulders. "You'd have to ask them, but it is not hard to guess they are willing to risk it. What we found here is too important for them to let go."

"How did they even know about this? Who told them?"

"News of the discovered ruins on Epsilon is not exactly a secret."

"Yes, ruins from ancient reptilian races."

Yules chuckled softly. "There are giant reptiles roaming the surface of this planet. That it was once inhabited by an intelligent race of Reptilians is not hard to guess. Don't fool yourself, Turner. The Dragons know about the forgotten sanctuaries the Spiders built a hundred thousand years ago. They also want the technology that comes with their discovery."

"Epsilon belongs to the Humans. This technology is ours."

"It belongs to its rightful owners...the Spiders." Yules turned away and followed Mirna, who had disappeared in the darkness of the cave.

Clayton clapped Turner on the shoulder. "Cheer up, friend. There is nothing you can do about this. Let it go and let it run its course. The Spiders are not evil. They may not look like us on the outside, but inside we are all brothers and must try to live together in harmony. This universe is big enough for all of us. Come on and let's see what else we can discover."

As they walked across the smooth floor, they saw a nearly impossible number of the transparent containers filled with black Spider eggs. Turner tried to estimate their number but gave up after a while. He became aware of a sudden droning sound reverberating through the cavern.

Before he could ask, Clayton said, "They've begun drilling."

"What exactly is happening here?"

"The Spider robots are drilling a hole through the ceiling. They'll install an elevator and then they will transport the eggs into the hatchery."

"You seem excited about this."

"How could I not be? This is a monumental event. Just think about it. These eggs have been in suspended animation for over a hundred thousand years and they will be brought back to life. The parents of these young Spiders lived a thousand centuries ago. The universe was different then. Temperatures on Earth were beginning to cool. Homo sapiens roamed the South African continent, using simple tools and hunting with primitive weapons, while the Spiders and the Dragons traveled the Galaxy in spaceships and fought a war with weapons capable of destroying whole planets." Clayton spoke with an enthusiastic voice. "In the eyes of Humans these races were gods."

"Or devils." Turner had to admit, it did sound exciting…if you were a member of the Spider race or a scientist. He was neither. He was only a man who wanted nothing more than get off a planet that had kept him prisoner for five years.

He had nearly forgotten his original purpose for coming to Epsilon, forgotten about the Belter's Secret Service, the PIA, who sent him here as a spy to find out the truth about the Solar Union and the Trading Commission, and to find a way to break their monopoly on a planet full of treasures.

The Belters were not interested in emeralds and sapphires. They needed and wanted the drugs and medicines the jungle on Epsilon produced. This planet was important to their survival. They could not let the Spiders have it.

"You are a Belter," he said to Clayton as they walked on.

"Sure am."

"Are you not concerned about the survival of your people?"

"By *your people* you mean the Belters, I suppose. What are you getting at?"

"We need Epsilon. We need the drugs to cure the epidemic caused by living in low gravity conditions. If the Spiders claim Epsilon that will all be lost. Many of our people will die. Do you want that on your conscience?"

Clayton gave out a short laugh. "You know as well as I that the Solar Union controls the export of drugs and precious stones. We have to pay dearly for anything we import. Would it make much difference if we trade with the Spiders instead of the Union?"

"The Spiders may not want to trade. Besides, if there is a war between Humans and Spiders, Epsilon could be destroyed in the conflict. Think about that!"

"It won't happen, don't worry about that." Clayton spoke with confidence.

Turner did not share his confidence and he made up his mind to do whatever was necessary to stop these eggs from hatching and to stop the Spiders from reclaiming their lost knowledge.

The cavern ended and made a sharp turn. As soon as they took the turn, Turner saw a light ahead. He realized it came from Mirna's and Yules's headlamps. The new cavern didn't hold any containers with

Spider eggs. It was filled with rows of large spheres…their purpose a mystery to Turner.

When they reached Mirna and Yules, she gave them a happy smile.

"What are those?" Clayton asked.

"Spacecraft," Mirna said. "Each one is manned by a robotic entity." She paused. "They are ready to be deployed."

"Are they armed?" Turner asked.

She nodded. "Yes, they are. Each craft is an intelligent fighting machine, capable of traveling in space and able to make its own decisions. My ancestors were a warlike race."

"And now?" Turner looked into her face, trying to read her expression. She looked the same; her mannerism had changed back to the way she had behaved before she revealed her true identity.

She chuckled. It was difficult for Turner to imagine her mind was the alien mind of a Spider.

"Now?" she said. Then she shrugged. "We have evolved. We are as peaceful as the human race."

Turner stared at her, not knowing if she was speaking sarcastically. "That is reassuring," he said. "Most reassuring. What about the ones who will hatch from those eggs? They are a hundred thousand years old. How peaceful are they?"

"Their mentality may be unlike ours, but they will grow up and educated in a different environment."

"And these war machines? They were programmed by your warlike ancestors. How will you control those? Can you control them?" He didn't want to think about the electronic minds inhabiting the big black spheres, but they looked ominous and their existence represented a threat to the human race. He was afraid what kind of monsters would awaken should they be revived. He could not let that happen.

"They will not be activated unless it is necessary," Mirna said. She looked at an instrument she carried on her wrist. "It is near midnight. I suggest we get some sleep. We might as well bed down here."

Turner realized suddenly how tired he was. They had been on the move since they left the Spider camp, fought the jungle, and battled with large and small dinosaurs, with little rest in between.

He used his backpack as a pillow and closed his eyes, but not before he made sure his flash rifle was within easy reach.

* * * *

A booming sound ripped him out of his sleep. Opening his eyes, it took him a moment to orient himself. A second boom made him sit up. The others woke up at the same time he did.

"They've broken through," Mirna said

All four of them ran back to the first cavern. They could feel a sudden warm draft rushing through the cavern and then they saw light spilling from a hole in the roof at the far end.

Turner watched as a number of Spiders dropped out of the hole onto the ground. They came scuttling toward Mirna and the three Humans. Turner's first impulse was to fire his flash rifle into the gray bodies, but he suppressed it. He told himself he had nothing to fear from them. They were robotic beings. They would not kill him and devour him. At least that's what he hoped.

Mirna walked up to them. Turner didn't hear anything, but he knew she was conversing with one of the spidery creatures. After a while they left and disappeared through the hole in the ceiling. He watched as they scampered up the walls and ran across the ceiling.

"We've done our job. Now it is up to the working crew to do the rest. They'll be lowering a basket down for us so we can get to the surface. I don't feel like walking back the way we came. Too many obstacles along the way." Mirna gave Turner a long look. "I'm not sure what to do with you. You've been a great help in locating an entrance that led us here, but that ended your usefulness." Her lips opened to reveal her thin fangs. "Will keeping you around just so I can drink your blood be enough reason to let you live?"

Turner took a step backward, his hand tightening its grip on his flash rifle. "I came to you for help, that's all I wanted from the start," he said. "You promised me help in exchange for information. I kept my bargain and I expect you to keep yours. You are in no danger from me."

"How can I be certain of that? The moment you'll be back with your people you will be a threat to us and to this project. No one must know about this habitat and its purpose on this planet. There is too much at stake." Her eyes glowed faintly as she studied him. "You are under my control for now, but it won't last forever."

He felt spidery fingers touching his mind as he looked into her jade-colored eyes. The stirring in his loins made him conscious of his sudden hunger for her. Involuntarily, he took a step forward.

She laughed and closed her eyes for a moment. "Not now," she said softly.

The desire fell away like a cloak when they broke eye contact. He gripped his weapon, aware of the beads of perspiration pearling on his forehead. He realized he needed to get away from her. Sooner or later she'd get tired of playing games, and she would kill him. It would be easy for her when he lay in her arms, crazed with lust and the craving for the ecstasy he found in her embrace.

She turned and walked away. He watched her swaying body, torn with emotion. His rifle felt heavy in his hands. One burst from it would end her existence and remove the danger she represented, but his freedom would be short-lived. If Yules or Clayton didn't shoot him, the Spiders would surely tear him apart. The ones present were only automatons, but they would see a threat in him and eliminate him.

If they didn't, they would alert their masters and it would be only a matter of time until he would be punished for his crime. Mirna was a member of the Spider race, even if she didn't appear as such.

The basket touched the ground and they climbed into it. When they reached the surface, Turner squinted into the bright morning sun as it burned with a blazing fire above the mushroom umbrellas surrounding the valley.

A giant machine loomed above the hole that led into the caves below. The Spider robots were already busy dismantling the drill and some of them began installing other components. Turner assumed they were building the elevator, which would bring the black eggs up to the surface.

He marveled at the efficiency the gray beings displayed. The Humans had builder robots, but these were superior to anything Turner had ever seen. He realized having the Spider race for an enemy would be disastrous for the Human race.

Mirna touched his arm. "Come," she told him. "It is time for me to feed. I will decide what your future will be."

Turner tried to fight her influence, but he could not resist her allure. He followed her meekly as she pulled him with her. He threw one last look at Yules and Clayton. He wanted to say *Don't let her murder me* but no words came across his lips. The pounding in his loins overrode his fear and turned him into a mindless creature consumed by lust and uncontrollable yearning for Mirna's scorching passion.

Both men seemed to watch with amusement in their eyes and he knew he could expect no help from them.

* * * *

He was still alive. Mirna had not killed him during their savage encounter…not yet. She had shown him her feral side, the one that didn't care about his satisfaction, the one bent on one thing only…to feed.

It seemed once her hunger had been stilled, she suddenly changed and gave him what he craved. He called out hoarsely as he experienced his first orgasm and lost himself in her passionate and furious lovemaking. At times she rode him with great vigor, at other times she knelt in front of him and let him pound away between her soft buttocks, arching her back to take him deep into her.

He lost all sense of time or purpose. He only existed to fuck this ferocious creature. Fuck her until he dropped from exhaustion. He was nothing more than an animal in heat.

She turned onto her back and watched him with jade-colored eyes as he fell between her spread thighs. Looking into her beautiful face, it was hard to think of her as an alien being. He couldn't figure out exactly what she was. She told him she had been artificially created by the Spiders to look like a Human. Did that make her human on the inside also or was she technically still a Spider? He didn't know and didn't care. Right now, as she moved under him, she acted like any human woman. She was passionate and almost loving, cried out when her body was in the throes of an orgasm and sighed deeply when it was over.

He dug his fingers into her buttocks when he felt another climax approaching. Shouting savagely, he released the built-up pressure. She let out a growling sound, like that of a wild animal. When he looked into her eyes, he saw them change, take on a glow that made them even more alien. Her mouth opened, displaying her needle-thin fangs. With a fierce howl, she sank them into his neck. There was no pain. To the contrary…the joy he experienced in her arms as he climaxed inside her clutching vessel, increased to a level that made it nearly unbearable. Darkness descended and he drifted in a void filled with pleasure and pain.

When he regained awareness, he was alone.

Sitting up, he found himself lying on a cot, naked, in a room he recognized as Mirna's. His clothes lay on the floor in an untidy heap.

Slowly, he slipped from the cot and dressed. He felt tired and drained, but he was alive. For how long, he didn't know. Perhaps next time she would kill him.

He knew he needed to get away from this place and from her...to save his life and his sanity.

It was daylight outside. The builder robots had been busy all night. It seemed the elevator into the cavern below was finished. He saw them carrying containers filled with black eggs out of the elevator and into the habitat.

There was something else that caught Turner's attention.

Beside the habitat sat a large black ship. It must have landed during the night, because he didn't remember seeing it there when they came out of the shaft. As he watched, smaller vessels floated out of a gaping hole in the side of the large ship, like offspring leaving the birth canal of a giant alien creature.

The smaller vessels, clearly shuttles, settled silently on the moss-covered ground. They were teardrop shaped, only large enough for the pilot and possibly two or three passengers.

Human passengers, but he doubted that these shuttles had been built by Humans...or for Humans. He had never seen shuttles of such design.

"I see you survived the night."

Turner swiveled his head to look at the speaker. Grinning sourly, he touched his forehead with his closed fist in the greeting of the Belters. "You look surprised, Clayton."

"I'm only speaking metaphorically. Mirna won't kill you, not on purpose. She needs you to feed."

"I wouldn't be so sure. She is an alien creature, Clayton. You can't know how she thinks."

"She's been with us long enough. We know her."

"She may look like a human woman, but her mind is an alien. How can you say you know her?"

"We do, trust me."

Turner's gaze wandered over to the huge black ship. "What is that ship doing here?"

Clayton shrugged. "We are not sure. They are not consulting with us. It seems we've done our job. Now they are taking over."

"Aren't you afraid you'll be eliminated?"

"No. We have a deal with them. As I told you in the cavern, many colonists deal with the Spiders. We know they can be trusted."

"Don't be so sure. The Spiders are not human. They look different on the outside…they are different on the inside."

"You may be surprised how similar our races are." Clayton gave Turner a thoughtful look. "You must have noticed Mirna's different moods. Are they so different from ours?"

"No, they are not. Mirna is an enigma to me. It is hard to think of her as a Spider." Turner looked again at the big ship. "I don't trust them. I'm afraid the presence of that ship is a bad omen. What is the purpose for all those shuttles?" He counted ten aircraft resting on the blue-green moss, like ten giant glittering drops of oil, left there in two neat rows by an unseen giant for some unholy end.

When he saw humanoid figures leaving the large ship, he wondered even more.

"What are those?" he asked Clayton.

"Spiders."

"You mean like Mirna? But they don't look human."

"Not these. They are reptilian."

"Why are they here?"

Clayton shrugged again. "Don't know, but I'm sure we'll find out soon enough." He slapped at a pesky insect intent on landing on his nose. "This planet with its inhabitants is beginning to irritate me," he cursed. "Insects as large as birds, giant lizards crapping all over the place, polluting the ground and the air. And the mushrooms…I've never liked mushrooms. The sooner my mission is over the sooner I can get back into space."

"If the Spiders let you," Turner said sarcastically.

"They will, don't worry about that. You know, maybe it's time Humans learn to live with their neighbors in space. Humans are the newcomers here, not the Spiders, or the Dragons. Humans should learn a little bit of humility and not come upon the scene blistering and shooting guns, acting as if they own the universe."

"Now you talk like one of them. I'm beginning to doubt your humanity. Perhaps inside, you are also a Spider. Besides, we're not the ones invading a planet already claimed."

"Are you so sure about that? Maybe we are the intruders. Ever think about that?" Clayton pointed to the ground. "The Spiders were here long before us. Those eggs we found prove it. And so were the Dragons."

"Be it as it may, right now I'm not worried about politics or the history of the universe. I just want to get the hell away from here before your friends decide to kill me." His eyes locked with Clayton's. "If they are so friendly, why won't they just let me walk out of here?"

Clayton let out a small chuckle. "You were the one who came to us for help, remember? You were the one lost in the jungle."

"Not lost. I have no means of getting back to my camp."

"You still don't."

"There are ten shuttles parked over there. Surely, they could spare one to take me back home."

"You know that won't happen. All I can say is, be patient, don't antagonize anyone, and everything will turn out right. Trust me and don't worry so much." Clayton turned away. "I'm going hunting. I feel like broiling some dinosaur steaks tonight."

Turner watched him walking toward the jungle, his flash rifle across his shoulders. He envied the man right now. Clayton didn't seem to care about what was going to happen to Epsilon. He didn't worry about politics or the welfare of anyone on this planet or anywhere else. His only concern was to fill his stomach and enjoy a good meal.

Perhaps that was the way to be. Turner spent five years on this planet. It was his home. Deep down he had to admit that he loved the jungle, loved the violent environment and the ferocious beasts inhabiting it, but he had not forgotten his reason for coming to Epsilon.

The stranglehold the Trading Commission had on the export of goods needed to be broken. Epsilon's jungle didn't harbor only dangerous beasts and poisonous plants. It also produced drugs and medicinal plants, which were desperately needed by the Belters...his people. The abundance of gems was a bonus and of value only to treasure seekers and fortune hunters, but they boosted the economy and created wealth. Unfortunately, only for the people who owned the Trading Commission. That situation was wrong and in need of being corrected.

He watched the group of humanoids and wondered about their purpose for being here. Things were about to change on Epsilon, he had no doubts about that, but would the changes be beneficial to the Humans? He doubted that also.

The need to get away from here was stronger than ever. He'd have to find a way to sneak out of the camp undetected. And there, unfortunately, lay the problem. He'd never make it back home alive, not in the jungle, not alone and not without better transportation.

The loss of his pack animal had put limits on his mode of travel. With its webbed feet it had been able to move across swamps and areas of quicksand, places he had to skirt now. It added distance to his travels and took him into areas unknown and filled with dangers.

Raptor's Tooth was about seventy miles to the southeast. Not far with a scooter or sitting on the back of a Boraz, but virtually unreachable when traveling on foot through a jungle populated by fierce lizards of all shapes and sizes...all of them hungry. In addition to that, he would need his pack and flash rifle, which were inside the shuttle. It would look suspicious should he carry both of them outside and wander off into the jungle.

The arrival of the Spider ship with its cargo increased his need to leave their camp as soon as possible, but he knew they would not permit it. Whatever they planned, they could not afford a Human to announce their presence.

Of course, the watchers in the Outpost probably already had registered the intruder into the system. Possibly, anytime now a ship would come to investigate.

He could only hope.

In the meantime it may not hurt to study the newcomers a little closer. Slowly, he wandered toward the big ship and the group of humanoids. He tried to calculate their numbers and estimated about thirty. Three for each shuttle. One pilot and two passengers.

A few of them noticed his presence and observed his approach with watchful, glittering eyes. As he came closer, their reptilian appearance became apparent, but he also realized they were of an unfamiliar race. Of course, there were many different species and not all had been encountered by Humans. They wore only loose pants, no garments to cover up their upper bodies. Most of them were females; he saw only a few males.

All had superbly built bodies. The males were muscular and the females slim with lovely-shaped bodies. Had it not been for their light-green shimmering skin, they could have passed for Humans. Almost…until one took a closer look. Their bald heads were round and covered with dark scales.

He didn't know if they spoke any of the Human languages, since their bodies had been created reptilian, so he just lifted his open hand in greeting, hoping they would not mistake it for a hostile gesture.

A couple of them imitated him. They smiled, exposing small, triangular shaped teeth. It didn't really surprise him to see long, needle-thin incisors. One of the males approached him and touched his neck. His fingers felt soft and warm. He turned around and said something in a hissing language to his compatriots. They let out sounds that could only be laughter.

"I wish I understood the joke," Turner said.

The alien with his fingers on Turner's neck exposed his teeth and hissed. Then he said, "There was no joke. I told them your blood pulses strong in your veins."

Startled to hear him speak Inglis, Turner said, "Why are you so interested in my blood?" He guessed the answer and was not surprised when the alien said, "They told us we'd be able to feed well."

Turner looked at him coldly, "If you try to sink your teeth into my neck it may be the last thing you do, my friend." He touched the gun on his hip.

The alien laughed. He crooked a finger at one of the females. She smiled and came over, hips swinging. Her fangs gleamed white between her purple lips. The male said something to her in their language, which made her emit a series of high-pitched sounds. She approached Turner and pressed her naked upper body against his. Her breasts felt soft and he could feel the heat from her body even through his shirt. Her eyes were level with his, which was no big feat, since he was only five foot six. In fact, the thin, dark-green membrane rising up from the center of her skull, like the comb of a rooster, created the illusion she loomed over him. Her slightly protruding eyes had slit pupils, like the eyes of a poisonous viper. They glowed with yellow fire under the bony ridge of her brow.

He felt a pulling in his head and became aware of a sudden gentle fluttering below his belly. He closed his eyes and moved away from her. She laughed and followed him. Putting a hand behind his neck, she pulled him close and pressed her lips on his, forcing her tongue between his teeth. The twin ends of her tongue probed the inside of his mouth for one short moment. Then, with a quick movement, she moved her lips onto his neck and licked it with a wet tongue. He felt sharp teeth on his artery, but they didn't penetrate his skin.

Pushing him away with an abrupt, forceful shove, she said, "You will not be able to resist me, puny Human, should I feel the need to drink your blood." A loud hiss escaped her open mouth and her long, split tongue darted in and out, like a pair of provoked serpents.

Turner stood immobile and watched her stalking back to the group. The others regarded him with their yellow eyes, a bemused smile upon their lips.

"What do you want here?" he asked with a rough voice, every fiber of his body telling him to turn and run, but he was too stubborn to follow the impulse.

The male he had first spoken to made sharp, gurgling sounds. Running a hand over his mouth, he said, "We came to feed."

His words froze the blood in Turner's veins. He felt suddenly cold inside, even though the air was beginning to heat up as the day progressed.

"I hope you like Dinosaur steaks," he said through his teeth, his mind made up. Swinging around, he headed back to the shuttle and boarded it. He went to get his pack and shouldered it onto his back. Grabbing his flash rifle, he left the shuttle and turned toward the jungle. He had no idea where Mirna and Yules were hiding out, but at the moment he didn't care. He only hoped nobody would miss him until he was far away from the Spider camp.

When he entered the protection of the jungle, he breathed a sigh of relief. Looking back, he didn't see anyone following him. He didn't know what kind of tracking devices they had, but he trusted the jungle to hide him...as long as he could get far enough away without being detected. They would have to follow him on foot and he trusted his knowledge of the jungle to keep ahead of them.

Of course, the Spiders were not his only problem. Now he faced other dangers, but he hoped his ability to spot dinosaurs and his luck would keep him from becoming the victim of one of the roaming hungry beasts.

The sun was visible through the mushroom umbrellas and he used it and his watch to determine the southeast direction, utilizing his compass only as backup and to confirm he was on the right track.

He didn't follow the same trail they had traveled only two days before. If they were smart, they would go back underground and try to cut him off before he reached the entrance to the underground cavern, since they could travel so much faster underground. But they didn't really know which direction he would take and most likely wouldn't waste their time chasing him that way. In any case, he'd make certain he did not end up near that part of the jungle and they'd probably guess that also. Maybe they would just forget about him and hope he would perish in the jungle.

It was a small hope to cling to.

By nightfall he was quite certain nobody was following him. So far, he had not encountered any large predators, not even any Raptors, and he was grateful for that. Before it became too dark to travel, he searched for an Octopus tree and crawled into the mass of roots, taking care to check for other denizen of the jungle that may have taken refuge under the giant tree. Sometimes a family of *Lice* would set up residence among the roots. They were not aggressive and usually avoided other creatures, but they could inflict painful wounds with their long, needle-thin trunks when they felt threatened.

Luckily, there were no other tenants under the roots and, using his pack as a pillow, he made himself comfortable for the night. The soil he lay on felt sticky from the secretions of the roots and smelled a bit unpleasant, so he put on his air filter. He adjusted his insect repeller to its highest setting, hoping the high-pitched sounds it emitted would also keep other interested parties away from his hiding place.

He froze and held his breath when he heard the growling of a predator near the entrance to the small cave under the roots. Seeing the glint of yellow eyes staring at him through the tangle of roots made his heart beat faster and he gripped his flash rifle with sweaty fingers. The owner of those eyes was large and most likely hungry.

Chapter Six

The intruder finally moved on, but after that Turner didn't sleep soundly. The noises of the night-roamers and his fear Mirna and her new companions would search for him kept him awake.

When morning came, he felt tired and hurt in numerous places. Before crawling into the open, he made certain the area outside was clear of any hungry critters that may be waiting for breakfast. He took off his helmet and shook out the dirt that had seeped into it during the night. Feeling pangs of hunger, he searched among the ferns growing around the base of the tree and was lucky to find a small nest of *Rootbeetles*. They tasted excellent roasted. Not wanting to waste any time he ate them raw. Sucking the juice from a couple of *Fernapples* supplied him with liquid. Then he was ready to move on.

He could see the light of the sun creeping through the roof of mushroom umbrellas and noted the direction of the shadows to get his bearing. When he checked in his pack, he discovered the crude map he had drawn and studied it. There was a large swamp ahead of him and he decided to change direction so he would miss it. This time he would not trespass the territory of the Eer because their hive lay further west. Perhaps he should have searched them out again and asked for their help, but there was no guarantee the warriors and hunters would have taken him back to their hive and he didn't know if he would have been able to communicate with them.

Constantly alert for any signs of large or small predators, he followed a narrow path through the ferns and shrubs, hoping the path would not change direction too often. When it did, he used his machete to cut his own path until he came upon another one. There were many such trails and most of the time he didn't have to exert himself too much hacking at the occasionally tough vegetation. He avoided the wide trails, knowing from experience they sometimes held unpleasant surprises. One of the larger carnosaurs might just decide to wait for its next meal, lying flat and motionless in the middle of the trail until it was too late for the intended victim to flee.

Once he came across a small herd of *Rock Ants*. They looked like their large cousins, the Uur and Eer, but these were the equivalent of monkeys versus Humans on Earth when it came to intelligence.

They were not warlike or aggressive, but it was still a good idea to let them pass by with as little attention as possible. Their mandibles were sharp and strong enough to inflict serious wounds.

Turner stepped off the trail and moved further into the protection of the underbrush. He waited until they were gone before he resumed his journey. They had probably been aware of him, but had not perceived him as a threat or considered him food. As far as he knew, they were vegetarians. But on Epsilon one could never be sure of anything.

By noon he had traveled farther than expected but did not relax. Should Mirna and the others decide to search for him, they could use one of the newly arrived shuttles and could easily overtake him. The deeper he made it into the jungle away from their camp the greater the circle they would have to search in hopes of locating him.

The hot, humid air made him feel uncomfortable and he kept an eye open for a chance to cool down. When he heard the gurgling noises of running water across rocks, he followed the sound and discovered a shallow stream with crystal-clear water. The stream was narrow enough not to hide anything nasty, but experience had taught him never to drop his guard.

He dipped his hands into the water and found it cool. Cupping his hands, he scooped some up and took a few careful sips. It tasted good and he drank more. After refilling his canteen, he washed his face and wet his hair, enjoying the refreshing coolness on his skin.

Feeling tired, he decided to take a break and rest for a while. This place was as good as any other place.

Making certain there were no other thirsty visitors nearby, he shrugged off his pack and sat with his back against the trunk of a mushroom tree, his flash rifle beside him, ready to be picked up should the need arise.

Even though he was tired and tempted to close his eyes and take a little snooze, he fought the urge. Falling asleep in the open like this could be a deadly mistake. Even a small predator represented great danger and could rip out his throat before he'd wake up.

When he heard the soft droning above, his eye flew open and he realized he had drifted off. Cursing, he rose and looked around him, panicking a little and angry for being so careless. The droning sound was still there and he recognized it for what it was.

A shuttle. They were looking for him.

A sudden pulling in his head made him drop his rifle and put his hands against his temples.

Damn it!

Mirna.

He remembered Yules's words…

She injected a substance into you, which lets her take over the motor functions of your body if she feels like it. The price you pay for the pleasure she bestows on you. She'll find you wherever you are. You can't hide from her.

She knew he was down here. It was just a matter of time before she found him.

He fought the impulse to run, fought the terrible pressure inside his head. He had come this far. He would not let her find him, but there was no place to run.

When he saw the shimmer of red on one of the shrubs on the other side of the stream, he knew what he must do. It would not be pleasant, probably dangerous, but it might be the only way to keep Mirna from locating him.

He jumped across the stream and stripped a handful of the red berries from the soft branches of the *Bloodberry bush,* shoved them into his mouth. They tasted awful, puckering the inside of his mouth, but that was nothing compared to what ingesting them would do to him. Only a desperate man or someone trying to commit suicide would even resort to eating the berries.

Turner was a desperate man.

He looked around for a hiding place, one that would keep him safe for the next three or four hours. He found it in the trunk of a mushroom tree. His first impulse was to run to it, but he had enough sense left to pick up his backpack and rifle.

The first painful flashes stabbed through his body and brain. There was not much time. Stumbling toward the giant mushroom, he fell and nearly passed out, but his will to live kept him conscious. Crawling on all fours, pulling his pack and rifle with him, he managed to reach the tree. Squeezing his aching body through the narrow opening, he collapsed into the tiny cave inside the trunk. His head was spinning, threatening to explode. The terrible pain roaring through his mind and body nearly drove him insane. He couldn't formulate any clear thoughts…

…Awareness came back with sudden clarity. He found himself sitting in a cramped position inside a dark place. His pack blocked the entrance to the small crevice in the trunk of the mushroom tree, restricting most of the light from seeping in. There was barely enough room for him to move around. Listening, he didn't hear anything outside. Carefully, he pushed the pack through the opening and stuck his head out, still listening for anything that might pose a threat to his safety.

Satisfied everything appeared safe, he crawled outside, pulling his rifle with him, ready to use it. Checking his watch, he noticed four hours had passed. He had guessed that much by the position of the sun, which he could see through openings in the roof the mushroom tops formed above him.

There was not much daylight left, but he couldn't afford to hang around. He was certain Mirna's shuttle was gone from the vicinity. The chances of her finding him again were slim since she didn't really know his destination.

He had a strange taste in his mouth from the bloodberries he consumed, but if that would be the only price to pay he'd be lucky. Sometimes there were unpleasant aftereffects. They usually were the results of eating too many. He hoped whatever aftereffects he might still suffer would be mild.

He thanked his lucky stars for finding the berries so quickly. Consuming them caused terrible pain, but they also possessed healing qualities, which outweighed the nasty side effects…in the appropriate circumstances. They were most effective for neutralizing the poison of venomous reptiles, of which there were plenty on Epsilon. Lowering a person's metabolism to a level close to death, they stopped the flow of poison into the bloodstream and gave the berries a chance to reduce the effects of the toxins.

They also stopped the activity of the brain.

Spending nearly five years in the jungle had taught Turner many things, mostly how to survive. A rumbling in his belly reminded him he was hungry. For a man who knew what to look for, there was no shortage of food. He spied a yellow-shimmering bush and dug around it with his machete. His efforts were rewarded when he found a number of black, oval eggs.

Moth-Eggs. They were nutritious and tasted delicious, even when eaten raw. He wolfed them down and topped off his meal with a couple of *candyplums*.

Checking his compass and map, he established the direction he wanted to travel, and moved on.

When it became almost too dark to travel any further, he searched for shelter to spend the night. He could use his headlamp to light his way, but the night also brought out the night-roamers, large and small, all of them unpleasant. In addition, the insects that cruised around at night were much more aggressive than their cousins which inhabited the jungle during the day. The light would, obviously, attract them by the thousands.

He found another Octopus tree and headed for it, when loud buzzing sounds stopped him in his tracks.

A few moments later dark shadows descended from above and blocked his way. He lowered his flash rifle and watched them with apprehension. They were as tall as Humans, but their semitransparent wings made them appear taller.

The first two were only about ten feet away from him. They regarded him with their multifaceted eyes, their spears pointing at him.

You are trespassing.

The words sounded loud and quite clear inside his head.

"It is not my intention to cause the Queel any trouble," he said aloud, knowing they would be able to pick up his thoughts. "I am only passing through on my way to my hive."

One of your flying vessels invaded our territory.

"It was not one of ours. It belongs to strangers, invaders, who will be the cause of unrest on Epsilon. I was their prisoner and I am trying to escape."

The Queel stayed silent for a moment. Then it said, *Your thoughts speak the truth. We will take you to our queen. She will decide your future.*

As they advanced their appearance seemed to change. He looked upon their perfect bodies. The spears of dim light the dying sun cast into the darkness made the wings sprouting from their wide shoulders glisten with blue fire and lend their handsome faces a god-like quality.

He knew his mind was playing tricks. This was one of the lingering consequences the bloodberries caused in his brain.

His rational mind shouted, "They are not human! This is nothing but an illusion! They are bees. Giant bees!"

Their eyes glowed softly as they looked at him, their lips smiling with certain arrogance. They knew what he saw, or thought he saw, but even knowing that didn't save him from his hallucinations.

They carried him with apparent ease into the upper regions of the jungle. Their main hive was built around the stem of a huge mushroom tree. Smaller hives hung from the gills of nearby mushroom umbrellas.

Turner didn't struggle, knowing it would be futile to resist them. Had they wanted him dead, they would have killed him by now.

They entered the hive through an entrance at the bottom and traveled through corridors and spacious rooms.

His hallucinating mind let him see handsome human males and beautiful human females and he wasn't certain if any of the other things he saw were real. His captors took him through winding corridors. He lost count of the many flights of stairs they climbed. When they finally emerged inside a garden, his mind was still rational enough to know that they were on top of the mushroom umbrella. The setting sun threw long shadows across a small pond, illuminating the nude figures bathing in the calm water.

Human figures.

This is an illusion! They are not real!

They watched him with interest as he stood under a tall shrub, his mind in turmoil. When he looked around he didn't see the warriors who had brought him.

"Why are you here?" a voice asked from behind him.

He turned to stare at the woman in a flowing robe. She was tall and beautiful. A thick mane of black hair flowed downed her shoulders in gentle waves. Her full lips were turned up into a mocking smile. The rays of the sun behind her showed the perfect lines of her body through the sheer material of her robe, making her appear naked.

He rubbed his forehead. "I'm...not sure what I'm doing here," he said haltingly, confused and lost for words. Even though his thoughts were sluggish, there was still enough rationality in his mind to realize that this could not be real. His mind was playing tricks.

She laughed throatily and came close. Standing in front of him, she looked into his eyes. "Reality is what you believe, Gilbert Turner."

"How do you know my name?"

Her finger touched his cheek in an intimate gesture. "It is in your thoughts." Her arm made a sweeping motion. "This is in your thoughts. It is real in your mind. I am real."

"You are only real inside my mind," he said. "It cannot be otherwise."

"What you see is real, only in a different form. Does it matter?"

"Are you human?"

"No."

"Who are you?"

"I am the queen of the Queel."

"Then you cannot look like a human being. This body I see is not real," he said stubbornly.

Her soft laughter mocked him. "My body is real. It is your mind that deceives you." Her hand reached for his. It felt warm and soft. "Come and sit with me, Human. Tell me your reason for being here."

They walked to a bench woven from branches and sat on it. He looked across the pond and noticed that the ones in the water were all females. Their bodies were perfectly shaped and their faces lovely and young. He turned his head to look at the queen. She sat silently beside him, studying him openly. Her gown had fallen open and he looked at the swell of her creamy breasts.

She smiled when she noticed his eyes. "Human males are fascinated by a female's breasts," she said. "I find that interesting. Why is that so?"

He shrugged. "I don't know. I guess it is part of our genetic makeup." He reached out gingerly and put one finger on her breast. "It feels soft."

"You can kiss it," she said. "I know you want to."

He bent over her and touched her breast with his lips. Her skin felt warm and satiny. He licked it with his tongue. Slowly, his mouth moved until he found her nipple. Taking it into his mouth, he sucked on it.

She pushed him away with gentle hands. "I am willing to give you what you crave, Gilbert Turner, if you will open your mind to me."

"How do I do that?" He stared at her, not understanding.

She stood and touched her gown. It opened and floated to the ground, leaving her naked. His breath caught in his throat when he studied the lovely lines of her body.

"You are beautiful," he said.

"Your mind makes me beautiful." She flowed to the ground and lay on the soft moss, looking up at him. "Come, Human, and join your body with mine. You will find me as passionate and responsive as a female of your own race."

The sun had disappeared, but one of the moons had risen. In its pallid light she looked like a vision out of a fairytale. The shrubs and small trees glittered with sparkling fire and threw soft shadows across her pale body, lending the whole scene a magical quality. Her arms reached for him, beckoned. Her legs bent and her thighs opened, exposing her female genitals to his view.

With shaking fingers he removed his clothing. When he was naked, he dropped to the ground and moved between her inviting open thighs. Her hand grasped his hard penis and stroked it gently. Pulling him closer, she guided him into her. Letting out a loud groan, he slid into her with ease and moved on top of her with erratic movements.

She responded and slammed her lower body against his, taking him deep into her with every thrust.

When he spilled his seed into her, he felt the ghostly finger of something touching his mind, but the bliss he experienced caused him to ignore it. He didn't care what she did as long as she gave him the satisfaction he craved.

* * * *

When he awoke, he found himself lying on his back, stark naked. Staring into the star-speckled sky, it took him a while to remember where he was. Memory rushed back almost painfully, making him sit up and look around. At first, he thought he was alone, but then he saw the figures bathing in the pond.

The faint light of the moon revealed the true nature of what floated in the water and he shuddered, remembering what had transpired only a short time ago.

One of them swam toward shore and climbed out. The body of the creature was outlined against the disk of the moon and what he saw left no doubt the creature was not human.

Staring at the giant Insectoid, he wondered how he could ever have mistaken it for a human being. His head seemed clear now, and he hoped all traces of the bloodberries had finally dissipated.

Had he not been naked he might have thought his memory could be false, possibly part of a dream, or wishful thinking.

What you remember happened.

Startled, he looked up. He had not seen the creature walk up to him.

"Are you...?" He didn't finish the sentence.

No. I am not the queen. I am one of her daughters. But I saw and observed. The outlines of her body began to oscillate, nearly disappeared. When it took form again, he saw a young, beautiful and quite naked young woman standing before him.

She smiled. "I am still learning how to manipulate other minds. I am not as good as the queen...not yet."

With the optical illusion also came the impression that she spoke audibly.

"How is it possible that you can make me see such a lovely human woman?"

"I take the image from you mind."

"Astounding." He studied her with curiosity. She reminded him of Geraldine Laymon, the woman he had spent some time with, only younger and more beautiful. The Geraldine who sometimes invaded his mind in his daydreams. The real Geraldine had been quite plain in appearance.

"I see you are beginning to understand," she said.

"Barely." He extended an arm and touched her shoulder. "Your body feels as soft as the body of a human woman. Your illusion is perfect." He looked into her soft brown eyes. "Tell me, why do you want to appear to me as a Human?"

"To make you feel more comfortable. My people have not had much contact with yours, but we are aware of you. We realize our world is changing. If we want to survive, we must adapt to the new conditions."

Turner nodded. "Tell me something else. Why did you mother, the queen, have sexual intercourse with me? Why did she seduce me the way she did?"

Her laugher startled him. She sounded so human. "When your body and hers formed a union, you let down your guard and left your mind wide open to her probing. It was the only way she could enter your mind fully and gain the information she was seeking."

"She could have asked me."

"Your short-term memory is of little value. She needed to have access to everything you ever experienced." Her eyes regarded him. "Would you have told her the truth about everything?"

"I don't know. Maybe."

"You are the first Human who has ever been inside our hive. When you leave here, you will take with you valuable information. What will you do with it?"

He shrugged. "Who would find usefulness in what I see and experience here?" Flashes of what happened between him and the Queel-queen shot through his mind. Did he want to broadcast that he had sex with a giant bee? It was probably best he pushed it into the deepest recesses of his mind, along with the memory of having had sex with the Eer-queen.

She must have followed his thoughts. Her hand touched his cheek. "You feel shame. Why is that?"

"I had sexual intercourse with a non-humanoid female…and not for the first time. It happened once before in the hive of the Eer. Many of my people will condemn me for that."

"You were drugged. You didn't know my mother wasn't human."

"Deep down I knew. I was just too horny to care. Perhaps my morals are all screwed up."

"Morals," she repeated. "That is a new concept. We have much to learn."

"As long as you learn the right stuff," he said. "We Humans carry a lot of baggage."

"I would like to join my body with yours so I can look deeper into your mind." She moved close to him and pressed her body against his. She felt soft and warm. Between his legs, his penis stirred, stiffened. "My sex-organ is as soft and as receptive as that of my mother," she whispered into his ear. Her lips moved across his cheek, touched his.

He moaned into her mouth and kissed her hungrily. They slid to the ground and within moments their bodies were locked together in a deep embrace. Her promise had not been empty. Her sheath felt like a satiny glove, and she moved under him with great vigor, her lower body whipping against his as he drove his organ into her. His mind swam in a sea of pleasure and ultimate joy.

* * * *

It was daylight when he regained his senses again.

He was alone. Even the pond was empty.

The sun had already begun its journey across the sky and was beating down on his exposed body. He found his clothing not far away in an untidy bundle, right next to a pile of heaped-up leaves and moss. He remembered sitting on a bench with the queen, but he didn't see it. He put on his pants and his shirt. Slipping into his boots, he found them almost too tight and was tempted to walk around barefoot. After a moment of hesitation, he put his helmet on his head and strapped his gun belt with his gun around his hip.

In daylight, his surroundings had lost their magic. In the stark light of the sun the shrubs and trees were nothing more than jungle vegetation. They did look trimmed, results of being tended by gardeners, alien gardeners…giant, intelligent bees, to be exact. The only thing making this park so unique was the fact it grew on top of a mushroom five hundred feet above the jungle floor. Taking a deep breath, he inhaled cool, almost dry air, much more pleasant than the humid, sticky air below the mushroom umbrellas.

He searched for his pack and flash rifle and was pleasantly surprised when he found both lying under a clump of ferns. More proof the Queel didn't mean him any harm. He was just about to go and pick up his belongings, when he saw one of the giant bees appear out of a hole in the ground. He stopped and watched the creature approaching him.

As he studied the creature, he noticed that *Giant Bee* was not really a correct description. It walked upright on two muscular legs, which strangely enough bent toward the front, like human legs. The lower part of the body was long, coming to a point at the bottom. It was connected to the upper half by an almost impossibly narrow waist. Between the juncture of the legs he saw a thick patch of golden fuzz hiding what could only be the creature's sex-organ…female by all appearances. The two long arms ended in hands with three fingers and an opposing thumb.

The face of the Queel was something out of a nightmare. The large, multifaceted eyes above an almost human-looking mouth gave the face a cold and rigid mask-like appearance. He didn't see a nose nor did he see anything resembling a nose. Two thin feelers above the eyes moved gently in a tight circle. Long, transparent wings sprouted from the creature's back. They hung like a nearly invisible cloak, their tips scraping the ground.

The Queel stopped in front of Turner. He discovered her lower body was covered with fine, yellowish down.

I am Spreeh. You and I joined our bodies under the moon.

"I didn't recognize you in the daylight," he said.

Her body wavered, changed. Then he looked upon the young woman who reminded him of his ex-lover Geraldine Laymon. Even in the bright light of the sun the illusion was perfect.

"Is this better?" she asked, a smile on her face.

"I'm not sure," he answered, studying her perfect naked body. Her breasts were larger than Geraldine's, her face more beautiful, and her body more voluptuous. As he looked at her he noticed a change coming over the body. Suddenly, she didn't appear as glamorous. She looked plain, ordinary. In fact, she looked exactly the way he remembered Geraldine.

"Is this better?"

Chuckling, he shook his head. "It doesn't really matter. I know what I see is not real. Whatever makes you comfortable." He stared into her human-looking eyes. "What is going to happen to me?"

She shrugged her shoulders. "That is not up to me to decide. The queen will decide your fate."

"Is there a chance I could be killed?" he asked bluntly.

She didn't answer for a moment. Her face didn't express any emotion. "I do not believe so," she answered after apparently pondering his question. "We do not kill our friends."

Her answer surprised him. "Are you saying I am a friend?"

"You have joined your body to that of the queen and to me, her daughter. You have opened your mind and we have looked into your thoughts. We know you harbor no ill feelings toward us. There is no reason to harm you. Yes, we are friends."

"Well, I am relieved to hear that." His eyes raked her naked body. "As much as I enjoy looking at you the way you are right now, I would prefer if you put on some clothing."

A slight shudder went through her body. "Like this?"

He nodded, amazed at the transformation he witnessed. The Queel, who called herself *Spreeh*, was dressed in a yellow, loose dress that covered her from neck to toes. "Much better," he said.

"I will show you how we live," she said. "When you report to the Humans who decide what happens on our world, you will tell them we are a peaceful people and we do not want to start any conflicts with the Humans."

"I will tell them, but you need not worry. We have contact with the Uur and we have never violated them."

"We know. That is one reason we did not kill you on sight." She put her hand on his arm. "Come now."

He walked beside her. When they passed the ferns where his pack and rifle lay, she said, "Leave them here. You won't need to carry them around. They'll be safe here until you leave."

She took him to the opening that led into the interior of the hive below. A tall mushroom with a large umbrella protected the entrance from rainwater running into the corridor and consequently into the hive. They climbed down a flight of stairs.

"Why do you need stairs to get from one floor to the next?" he asked. "Couldn't you just fly?"

"I could, but not all of our people have wings. There are the young whose wings are underdeveloped, and some of the worker classes have no wings at all. Many of the old ones loose the strength to fly and many get injured." She threw him a quick glance. "We do not abandon our weak ones."

"It seems you are more civilized than we assumed," Turner commented. "You have compassion. That is a commendable trait."

They walked down a long corridor. It seemed endless. The walls were dotted with round holes at regular intervals. He assumed they were apartments, much like the apartments in a building constructed by Humans. He never saw any doors. All the entrances to the rooms behind them were open. The corridor was lit up by softly glowing fungus covering the ceiling, but all of the rooms lay in darkness.

"What is behind those holes?" he asked.

"Rooms, but you know that. Your people live in an abandoned hive. You are not unfamiliar with the way we live. Most of the rooms are occupied by workers, who are gone during the day doing whatever they were designated to do."

"Don't the workers live with their families?"

She pondered the question for a moment. "Our society is structured differently from the society of you Humans. We don't have families in the way you do. Males and females do not live together. Females live in groups of families with their mothers. The males who have been selected to mate with eligible females live in groups headed by an older female, who teaches them the art of joining." She turned her head to look at Turner when he laughed. "Why are you laughing?"

"Don't you know? I thought you could read my mind."

"I can't read your mind all the time. Only when you are sexually aroused or when you are pondering something and your mind is troubled your thoughts are open to me." She gave a little laugh. "I am telling secrets," she said. "You haven't answered my question."

"Why I laughed? I thought it was funny that an older female teaches young males to have sex. Isn't the urge to have sex a natural function of any male?"

"Our males are not aggressive toward females. Mating with a female is something they need to be taught, just like the workers need to be taught how to do their job."

"Don't you have sex for fun?"

"For fun?"

"Yes, fun. Don't you enjoy having sex?"

"Oh, yes, we enjoy it very much, but we must be careful not to overpopulate the hive. That is one of the reasons the drones need to be taught how to do it properly without fertilizing the eggs inside a female. Only chosen females may deliver fertilized eggs."

"How do you know which of the hatching eggs will produce workers, warriors or males suitable for mating?"

"The designation of the hatchlings is determined after they hatch. Some are chosen to be workers, warriors, or members of other classes."

"Does that mean anybody can become a member of the Royal Family after…hatching?"

"No. Only the queen's offspring is classified as Royalty." They stopped in front of an opening. "Let's go in here."

They entered a large room occupied by young Queel sitting on cushions, apparently listening to a large adult standing in front of them. Turner assumed they were youngsters because of their small size. "What is happening here?" he asked.

"These young ones will someday be engineers. They are taught by a teacher." She looked at him. "Not much different from what Humans do, right?"

He nodded. "Not much. I just find it a bit odd since I don't hear anything. This class seems so silent."

"It isn't. The students are asking many questions. Remember, we don't have vocal cords like you. We talk with our minds."

"I keep forgetting because I can hear you talking."

"It is an illusion. I speak to you inside your head."

"Let me ask you a question. How do you know so much about Humans? I was under the impression that you don't have much contact with Humans."

"I received the information from your mind when you and I were one," she told him.

"Why don't I know anything about the Queel, other than what you are telling me and what I see? Shouldn't the process work both ways?"

"No, it doesn't because you don't know how to absorb knowledge from my mind. You do have the capability, but your mind needs to be trained."

They spent most of the day walking through the hive. He learned it took many years to tunnel all the corridors and rooms into the top of the mushroom tree. The smaller hives, which hung from the bottom of the umbrella, were residences of the Royal Family. The structures had been grown onto the tree through manipulation of the tree's natural fibers.

Turner was left with a great deal of respect for the Queel builders. He admired their ingenuity and skill to produce such a marvel of engineering.

Chapter Seven

As the day came to an end, Spreeh took him back up to the garden on top of the mushroom tree.

"It is still warm," she said, leading him to the pool. "Come into the water with me. It cleanses the body and spirit." Suddenly, she stood naked in front of him. He had not even noticed her transformation.

She laughed softly when she saw his astonished face. "I am getting better at this," she said. Then she turned and jumped into the water.

He could not comprehend the complete illusion she produced in his mind. Knowing he was watching a giant bee-like creature didn't change what he saw…a beautiful young woman with a perfect body swimming in the pond.

Shrugging, he undressed. There was no need to ponder it. *Might as well enjoy the water. It may be a long time until I'll have the chance again.*

He stepped into the pond, finding the water pleasant on his skin. Slowly submerging his whole body, he relished the feeling of joy he experienced. He couldn't remember the last time he enjoyed a bath like this. Anyone valuing his life never undressed fully in the jungle, never entered a pond, lake, or river on Epsilon. Never ever took a bath even in a harmless appearing stream. Too many dangers could lurk under the surface of the smallest pond or serene water surface.

Searching for Spreeh, he couldn't see her anywhere. He saw a small ripple on the water coming toward him and took a step backward when a sleek body shot out of the water right in front of him.

The creature looking at him with large, glittering eyes was humanoid but not human. He could see it was a female by the breasts on the scaly chest. Her face was alien but beautiful, even by human standards. Staring at the alien female he could see streams of water washing across green-shimmering soft shoulders as it was expelled from fluttering gills along the sleek neck.

"Spreeh?" he asked.

The alien female tilted her head. *I am not the one you are seeking.*

The voice sounded clear inside his head, but somehow he knew it was not Spreeh who spoke to him.

"Who are you? Another Queel?"

Silent laughter in his head. *I am not Queel. I am Soweia. My people live in the ocean.*

"In the ocean?" Turner tried to digest this new bit of information and its implication. It meant there were other races on Epsilon, races unknown to the Humans. The ocean was not a friendly place and nobody ever even entertained the idea it may be the home of intelligent beings. "Aren't you a little far away from your home?"

After a moment of silence, the creature let out an almost human sigh. *Yes, very far.*

He studied the slim body. "How can I be sure you are not just an illusion? How can I be sure you are not Spreeh or another one of the Queel females?"

The Soweia female shrugged. *You cannot be sure.* She came closer and touched his naked chest with a long finger. *What kind of creature are you? I've never seen anyone like you?*

"That makes two of us. Are there more of you?"

Yes. In the ocean. Far from here. My people are of a great number. Are there many of you?

"Yes, there are but not here on your world. I come from far away, much farther than where you live." He pointed into the sky. "I come from the stars."

Her round eyes became even rounder. *From the stars? Do you mean those lights in the night sky? How can that be? They are so small.*

He chuckled, amused by her childish innocence. "They only appear small from here. Those lights you see are balls of fire many times the size of your world. Many of them are surrounded by worlds like this one. Some of those worlds are covered by forests and oceans, some with nothing but water, and some have hardly any water. Others are cold with blankets of ice and snow and others are dry and dusty like the deserts on your world. As different as those worlds are from each other so are the beings that populate them. On the outside they are different from you and me. But the difference is only outside, because deep inside we are all the same. We live, we dream, we love, and sometimes we fight each other because we are different."

I don't want to fight with you. Her breasts grazed his chest as she came closer. Looking into his eyes, she asked, *Are you a male?*

"As much as you are a female." Feeling her soft breasts pressing against his chest and her nearness created in him a sudden desire to take her into his arms and kiss her full lips. In answer to his thoughts, she put her arms around his neck and pulled his head down until their lips touched. Opening her mouth, she pushed her tongue against his teeth. Surprised by her forwardness, he let her tongue enter his mouth. She tasted a little of seaweed and fresh spring water.

Her hand stole down his belly and when she touched his growing penis, he moaned and put his hands on her buttocks.

She broke the kiss but didn't push him away.

I've been lonely. I have felt a male's organ inside me only a few times and I am longing for the bliss it created inside my body. Are you capable of such a thing?

"I believe I am up to that." His penis had swollen inside her hand. "But I would prefer if we went on dry land. I'm not a creature of the water. I can't breathe under water."

I am a water-dweller, but I can breathe the air. If you carry me, I will come with you on land.

She let go of his member and he lifted her out of the water. She was not heavy, and he carried her easily on land. When he put her down in the soft moss, he realized why she asked him to carry her. She didn't have any feet. Her legs ended in flippers.

His eyes wandered to her genital area and he noted that her sex-organ was not much different from that of a human woman. She saw him staring and gave him a questioning look. *Is it possible?*

He lay down beside her and stroked her small breasts. "I don't see why not. There is only one way to find out." He kissed her gently and let his hand roam over her breasts.

She squirmed under his touch. *That feels nice.*

His hand moved across her belly down to her genital area. Stroking her thick labia with his fingers, he pushed one finger into her and found her slippery. She moved her lower body against his finger and moaned softly. Moving on top of her, he slipped between her spread legs. "Tell me if it hurts you," he whispered, proceeding to push his hard member into her offered orifice. He didn't know what to expect, but when he slid with ease into her, he let out a satisfied grunt and began to move slowly in and out of her.

She hugged him to her and moved her pelvis enthusiastically under him. Her breath came in great gasps and she let out small sounds of pleasure, proof that she was not an illusion but real flesh and blood. When she experienced her first orgasm, she emitted a series of shrill cries. He closed her mouth with a kiss and carried on with renewed vigor. Bringing her to a number of orgasms, he finally gave in to his body's demands and shot his seed into her, secure in the knowledge he didn't have to worry about getting her pregnant. She might be humanoid but there was an almost negligible chance their DNA would match.

He relaxed into her clutching arms and lay breathing hard on top of her. Her hands stroked his back gently and it felt good to have a soft, warm body underneath him. Somehow he knew she was real and not an illusion.

It was like I remembered. Did the Spirits of the Air send you to me to still my craving?

He chuckled into the valley between her breasts. "I could ask you the same question. I've been living a lonely life for many years now. Perhaps that is the reason why I am so easily seduced. This is really insane, you know. Maybe I'm insane and this is all just a crazy dream...the consequences of eating too many bloodberries."

I don't understand the meaning of your words.

He lay in the circle of her arms, not wishing this moment to end, hoping he would not wake up from a drug-induced dream. "It would take too long to explain. There is something else I'm wondering about...how did you get here? You claim to come from the ocean, and yet, here you are, living in a pond created by a race of intelligent Insectoids on top of a giant mushroom. How did you ever get up here?"

I was swimming too close to the surface when the Wind Spirits lifted me out of the water and carried me away. They dropped me softly onto the ground far away from my home. The Queel found me and brought me up here. They have been kind to me. She smiled and kissed him.

Her story made sense. The storms on Epsilon were violent and the winds capable of picking up objects to carry them for long distances. "You were very lucky you survived that ordeal," he said.

Lucky, yes, but I am lonely and long for others to keep me company. Will you stay with me?

"I'm afraid it is not possible, as much as the thought is tempting. It seems life up here is quiet and safe, not like the violence and danger waiting for me in the jungle. But I must get back to my people. Much is at stake here, even your safety."

She sighed audibly. *I feel sad about that.*

"So am I."

You must take me back into the water now. My skin is drying.

Reluctantly, he moved out of her embrace and lifted her off the soft ground. Then he carried her back to the pond and walked with her in his arms into the water where he put her down gently. She submerged for a moment and swam away from him. Then she came back. Rising up in front of him, she rubbed her body against his.

Thank you. Perhaps I will see you again?

"Perhaps. Nothing is impossible." He pulled her to him and kissed her gently. "I thank you for what you gave me. You've made my life a little less lonely for a while."

So have you. She looked at him one more time with her dark, glittering eyes and then she dove away, slapping her flippered feet onto the surface of the water to splash him. He watched her disappear into the dark depth.

Wading out, he suddenly wondered where Spreeh had gone. It was getting dark in the park and he seemed to be alone. The sun was close to the horizon and slowly disappeared below the treetops, washing the top of the jungle with red fire. With the sinking sun came the cold breeze.

He found his clothes and put them on. Not knowing what else to do, he searched for a comfortable spot where he could sleep. Out of habit, he scanned his surroundings, still not used to the idea that he could just lie down and sleep without worrying about being attacked and possibly torn to pieces by some hungry denizen of the night. Even the insects seemed to prefer the deep jungle to this idyllic place near the sky.

He whirled around when he heard a soft rustling, but it was only one of the Queel approaching him through the ferns, and he relaxed.

A familiar laugh inside his head made him recognize the queen's daughter.

"Spreeh," he said. "What happened to you? Where did you go after you entered the water?"

I made myself disappear from your mind. I wanted to give you a chance to meet the Soweia.

"We met." He squinted at her. "You arranged the meeting? I assume you knew what was going to happen?"

I put the thoughts into your head. I apologize for that. The Soweia was lonely and I wanted you to give her the pleasure you gave me.

"That was noble of you," Turner said, not knowing if he should be angry or grateful. After all, the young amphibian female did make him feel good. And it seemed he had stilled her longing for the company of a male, even if he wasn't a member of her species.

Do you want me to stay with you until the sun comes up again?

He was surprised by her question. "Are you asking me to have sex with you?"

No. I only want to keep you company. Her body became blurry and changed into the image of the human woman he had come to know. She was dressed in drab coveralls. He remembered Geraldine wearing coveralls like that.

"We can bed down over there. It will be comfortable." She pointed and pulled him to a spot under a mushroom with a wide umbrella. There was a small mound of soft moss piled up under it.

He felt suddenly tired and followed her invitation to lie down. She curled up beside him, her arms resting on his chest. "Sleep," she said softly. "Tomorrow you will leave our hive and go back to your people."

"Tomorrow," he murmured. "Yes. Tomorrow I will go home."

His dreams were filled with images of lovely amphibian females chasing him and trying to pull him under water and giant bees carrying him on their backs while they flew on their transparent wings high above the clouds. He awoke when a black ship shot out of the jungle into the sky and began throwing bolts of lightning at him. One of the bolts hit him in the chest and he fell through the clouds, screaming.

It was still night, but he could see by the color of the eastern sky that the sun was about to appear soon. Spreeh was still there beside him when he awoke, his body drenched with perspiration. Looking at her it dawned on him that he saw her in her natural form, proof she could only hold the illusion when she was conscious. He filed that information away for future reference.

He lay on his side, studying her and pondering his present situation. He was not appalled by the fact that in the last twenty-four hours he had coupled with a giant insect and an amphibian creature. At least they were both female, if that was a consolation.

Of course, before Spreeh and the Soweia he had sex with the queen of the Uur, a giant Ant, and Mirna, an artificially created humanoid with the mind of a Spider, a creature as far removed from the human form as was possible. He might as well have coupled with a Spider. The Queel in their natural form looked more human.

Thinking of Mirna made him wonder if she had given up her search for him. He also wondered about the Reptilians he had seen in the Spider Camp. What were they doing on Epsilon? Where they harbingers of what was ahead? Harbingers of turbulent times? He was certain their presence did not mean anything good.

Spreeh began to stir beside him. She moved her arm, which was still resting on his body. *You are awake already?*

"For quite some time," he said.

You have been studying me. Do you find me repulsive in my natural form?

"No, not at all. I find you…different. Attractive in an exotic way. I guess that is because you and I have been intimate sexually. Not only did our bodies join but also our minds. It's been a fascinating lesson for me."

For me also. You are the first male from another species who has entered my body with his productive organ. I found it stimulating and quite pleasurable. Her three-fingered hand reached out and stroked his cheek. *I will remember you with fondness, Human Gilbert Turner.*

"You will also stay in my memory, Spreeh."

The little park was suddenly bathed in bright light as the sun rose above the horizon. With the light came the heat. "I guess it's time to get up," Turner said. "You said last night I am going home today? It would be nice if I could just run across the treetops instead of having to get back down into the danger-filled jungle."

There will be no need for you to walk. I have designated six of our warriors to take you back to your people.

They rose from their resting place. Turner found his pack and slipped it on his back. Then he picked up his flash rifle. "I guess I'm as ready as I can be." A soft rumbling in his belly reminded him he hadn't eaten for a long time. He remembered seeing a Fernapple tree in the park, and when he looked around he found it again. It was covered with ripe fruit.

Spreeh saw his look and obviously read his mind. *Eat as many of the fruit as you like. They grow fast and taste delicious.*

"You eat them also?"

Yes. She laughed softly in his mind. *Finding pleasure in coupling is not the only thing we have in common.*

They both picked a few Fernapples and sat in the moss, eating them. For a moment Turner felt almost as if he were on a picnic…if he overlooked the fact his date was a female Insectoid instead of a human girl.

After eating, he picked up his pack and rifle again. Spreeh took him down through the maze of corridors and stairs. They finally ended up in a room that had a large opening in the floor through which he could see the vegetation far below the tree.

Four male Queel waited for them. Between them stood a contraption much like a chair with ropes.

These four will carry you safely to your people.

"I have a map where I want to go," he said.

That is good. You can explain it to them. They will understand. Now I must go back. She came up to him and put her long arms around him. While she looked into his eyes, she changed into human form. Her brown eyes studied him solemnly. "Have a good journey, Gilbert Turner. And a long life. We will meet again someday."

He pulled her to him and kissed her. "Live well," he said. Then he watched her walk away. As she walked, her image changed back into her natural shape. Her delicate, golden-shimmering wings trailed behind her like a veil and he could see her thin form through the thin membranes. Even in her natural form she was a beautiful, exotic creature.

He strapped himself into the seat and moments later the four Queel warriors carried the flimsy seat suspended by ropes high above the jungle floor toward the destination he gave them.

* * * *

Being carried high in the upper reaches of the jungle was quite an experience. The jungle looked different from high up. He saw a number of different species of dinosaurs hiding in the thick vegetation below, waiting for prey and he was happy to look at them from above instead of fighting his way through the ferns and the different varieties and sizes of mushrooms and vines.

Even the carnosaurs didn't seem so huge from his vantage point. But he knew that to be an illusion. He hoped the thin ropes supporting his seat wouldn't break and make him plunge to the ground into the open maw of a Rex or one of its hungry cousins.

Of course, he most likely wouldn't survive a fall from this height.

The four Queel who carried him did not appear to him as Humans but in their original shape. Their wings looked flimsy because of their near transparency, but they moved them with fast, powerful beats.

Two warriors, carrying spears, flew ahead of them, in case other, less friendly flying beasts made their appearance either from above or out of the lower branches of the giant conifers. He noticed that the other four Queel also carried spears.

There were many Queel in the upper and lower regions of the jungle. They went about a task he could only guess at. Probably collecting fruits and other items the Queel needed for their daily living. He likened their hive to a city where Humans resided. Or to a community inside an asteroid, which was probably a much better example. Everyone had a job to do. The Queel, the Uur, the Soweia, who lived in the ocean, and other, not yet discovered races on Epsilon, were not unlike Humans, even though their outer appearance was so different.

He remembered his own words when he explained the lights in the night sky to the amphibian female living in the pond on top of the mushroom. ...*as different as those worlds are from each other so are the beings that populate them. On the outside they are different from you and me. But the difference is only outside, because deep inside we are all the same. We live, we dream, we love, and sometimes we fight each other because we are different.*

His experience with the Queel was proof that there should never be a need for conflict. Civilized people, whatever their shape, color, or faith, could live together in peace. Of course, he knew these were only the wishful thoughts of an idealist. Not everyone wanted to live in peace. Greed, jealousy, the hunger for power, and the need to dominate, the sick desire to inflict pain and misery on others and the pure evil that possessed many individuals did not allow such peaceful existence.

Were the Spiders evil? If he had to judge by Mirna and the Spiders in reptilian bodies he met back at the Spider base he had to assume that was so. But then again, could he judge a whole race by only a few individuals? It was possible this was only a group of outlaws or mercenaries working for a company comparable to the Trading Commission. Humans knew next to nothing about the Spider societies. How many planets did they populate? How many different governments did they have? How many criminal organizations existed among them? How many greedy companies who cared only about making a profit existed even among the Spiders?

What about Yules and Clayton? Could they be considered evil? They were driven by a desire to make money, a motive strong enough to betray their own kind. Would they go as far as taking part in murdering their fellow Humans to satisfy their yearning for wealth? They had not lifted a finger to help him. Mirna could have killed him and they probably would not have cared. But then again, he was assuming. Mirna had not killed him, possibly never would have. They had known that and therefore not acted. Mirna had used him to still her own craving for sexual gratification and to drink his blood, which she needed to survive. Could he fault her for that? Did that make her an evil creature? He wasn't sure of anything.

He was torn from his musings when he heard a familiar and terrifying scream. A dark shadow swept through the umbrella tops and headed straight for him and his escort.

A Dactyl.

The giant flying reptiles usually stayed above the top of the jungle. They weren't very good fliers when too many obstacles blocked their flight, but sometimes one of the younger, smaller ones, dared to enter the upper regions of the trees. Especially if the trees didn't grow too close together. The ones with wide umbrellas created more empty space between the trunks, providing flying creatures with room to fly.

It was obvious to Turner, the Queel had seen the Dactyl before he became aware of it. The four who carried his chair went into a dive and dropped down fast while the two warriors rose to meet the flying predator. Turner craned his neck to see what was happening and witnessed the competence and prowess of the Queel warriors.

The Dactyl was hindered by its wide wingspan and its limited ability to maneuver efficiently between the massive mushroom tree trunks. Smaller and faster than the large reptile, the two warriors circled it with such great speed Turner could barely follow their movements. They used their spears to slice the thick membranes between the ribbings of the leathery wings, instead of stabbing them into the muscular body, which might have resulted in losing their spears.

The Queel used their intelligence as well as their strength to defeat an enemy larger and more ferocious than they. They would have been successful had it not been for a second Dactyl breaking through the mushroom umbrellas. This one was larger than the first on. When it saw the Queel it emitted a roaring scream and zoomed in for the attack. The two warriors fighting the smaller Dactyl were in obvious danger. They would not be able to fight their new attacker.

The four who carried Turner obviously came to the same conclusion. They dropped even lower and set the contraption carrying him on top of one of the smaller mushrooms. Then they let go of the ropes and took off to battle the second intruder.

Turner watched them with great interest and much apprehension. Should the warriors be disabled or even killed by the Dactyls he would be affected more than he liked to think about. Perched on top of a mushroom he was still at least a couple hundred feet above ground. Getting down unharmed would be a challenge if not impossible. He could probably make use of the ropes attached to the chair but they would not be long enough to let him climb down all the way.

When he heard a scrabbling noise behind him, he turned his head to see what caused the noise. What he saw made the blood curdle in his veins and, cursing loudly, he whipped out his gun, unable to get his flash rifle fast enough from his shoulder. The creature that had emerged from an opening in the top of the mushroom umbrella hissed and scuttled closer, its foot-long stinger raised high above its head, ready to sink it into Turner's body.

What unfortunate luck to have been set down on top of a Ghost-Scorpion nest. Usually, they lived underground, but sometimes they built their nests inside trees and the top of a mushroom.

He fired a bullet into the body of the advancing Scorpion, aiming for the soft area below the belly. As the creature nearly burst apart from the exploding bullet, another one crept from the same hole. Firing again, he saw two more coming out of another spot.

Twisting his body, he shot both of them before they reached him, but one of them came much too close for Turner to feel safe sitting strapped into the chair. The Scorpion lay just beyond his feet, sharp pincers still clicking angrily, its jointed tail shuddering. Working feverishly, he undid the straps that held him prisoner. He needed to get his flash rifle because he knew he couldn't fire his gun fast enough should a horde of them appear, as he knew they would.

He barely managed to get free and whisk his rifle from his shoulder when the first of many climbed onto the spongy surface under his feet. Turner was ready, feeling more confident now that he could move freely. He shot the creature before it even came fully out of its hole, blocking others from coming out. But they pushed their dead companion into the open and then they came one after another. Turner burned them as they came into view and soon the charred bodies were piling up around him.

He had no idea how the Queel warriors were doing, but subconsciously he was aware of the flying reptiles' shrill screams and knew the battle was still going on.

Finally, no more Scorpions came out and he lowered his arms and his rifle to take a breather. Surveying the carnage he caused, he realized he must have killed at least fifty of the dog-sized creatures. In a way it was a shame he could not take advantage of his victory. A few prospectors collected the poison from the stinger and sold it to the Trading Commission, who in turn sold it to pharmaceutical companies. There were few things on Epsilon that could not be sold for profit. Unfortunately, the only real profits were made by the Commission, not by the people who harvested this and other commodities while putting their lives in danger.

From the corner of his eyes he saw a large, dark body plunge past him. When he looked up, he saw only one of the Dactyls still sailing above him. Watching the giant winged reptile fluttering, it became evident that it was on the verge of losing the battle. Its movements were sluggish and it barely managed to stay in the air, mainly because of its shredded wings.

The Queel warriors didn't appear tired at all. They dashed in and out, and with every dash they left behind another rip in one of the wings. Watching them, he realized that his first impulse to help the warriors and shoot the Dactyl down with his flash rifle was not feasible. The danger he might hit one of the warriors instead was too great. He also realized that his help was not necessary. One warrior finally decided to give the Dactyl the deathblow. He flew above the reptile and shot down like a projectile, plunging his spear deep into the back of the Dactyl. The spear stuck and the warrior let go of it, but the great beast faltered, its wings collapsed and it tumbled past him, crashing through the thick vegetation until it hit the ground with a loud thud.

The warrior who had delivered the deathly blow followed it to make sure it was dead. Moments later he came back up, carrying his recovered spear

His four carriers came down and landed beside him. After looking at the dead Ghost-Scorpions one of them touched his shoulder. *You are a great warrior. May the spirits of the ones you have slain give you strength and courage until your spirit joins them.*

Turner stared into the multifaceted eyes. "Thank you for the compliment." He chuckled. "I was fighting for my life. I had no choice but to kill them all. Congratulations on your victory. The Queel warriors have my respect."

As you have ours.

He strapped himself back into the chair and they grabbed the ends of the ropes. Then they took to the air, carrying him with them.

The rest of the journey went without any further mishaps. He knew he was near Raptor's Tooth when he saw a couple of prospectors fighting their way through the thick vegetation below him. They never saw him and his escort, making him wonder how many times he had traveled through the jungle and never seen members of the Queel or any of the other intelligent indigenous people inhabiting Epsilon, even though they had been close by. He was certain they had always been aware of his presence.

The first habitat came into view. It perched high above the ground on top of a wide conifer tree branch. One of the prospectors had built it from branches and vines and then covered the whole structure with a coat of resin to make it impervious to water and wind. It wasn't large, barely roomy enough to house one person.

He often wondered why some prospectors chose to live in these cramped conditions when there were still plenty of spacious rooms available in the abandoned Queel hive used by the majority of Raptor's Tooth's inhabitants. Most of the ones who lived in their own, personal habitats were usually considered hermits by the others, but nobody questioned their desire to live alone without interference from anyone.

Turner's apartment was inside the hive. The Queel flew with him to the giant mushroom tree on which the hive had been built so long ago. They dropped through the upper branches of the conifers and past the umbrellas of smaller mushrooms. Letting the chair that held him settle softly onto the ground, they landed beside him.

A few people who had been busy with chores, watched with obvious amazement as he removed the straps holding him. At first they just stood further away and watched, but then a few of the men came closer.

"Is that some new mode of traveling?" one of them asked, staring at the Queel warriors who stood silent around the contraption that had carried Turner.

Turner laughed, throwing his pack on his back and shouldering his flash rifle. "These are my new friends," he said, indicating the Queel. He turned to them and said, "I thank you for what you've done. Tell your queen and her daughter Spreeh I will forever be grateful for your help. Without you I may have perished."

We will return to our hive with your message. One warrior lifted his hand. *Live well, Human Gilbert Turner.*

All six of them rose into the air at the same time, two of them carrying the now empty chair. Turner watched them disappear into the upper section above the smaller mushrooms before he turned back to the people who were crowding around him.

Chapter Eight

"How did you communicate with them?" one prospector asked. "Or didn't you?"

"Oh, I communicated alright," Turner said. "They are telepaths. They use their minds to talk."

"They never bothered with us before," another prospector said. "Why now? How did you convince them to bring you here in that...whatever that was?"

"It's a long story, my friends. Some of it is not pleasant." Turner looked at the anxious faces waiting for him to talk. "I'll arrange for a special meeting once I got some rest. Right now I'm exhausted and need a bit of sleep. By the way, for those of you who don't recognize me or don't know who I am, my name is Gilbert Turner. Make sure you all come to the meeting because it is important. What I have to tell you will affect each and every one of you."

"I thought I recognized you, Turner. Good to see you back alive," an old prospector said. "What happened to your Boraz?"

"Rex got 'em. Both of them." He shrugged. "Lady Fate is like that sometimes. I lost a few good gems too and some gear. This wasn't a very good trip." He slapped the other man on the shoulder. "Good to see you, too, Sinclair. I haven't seen you around for some time."

"Been busy." Sinclair grinned. "Me and Johnston were kinda lucky. Found some good stuff. Maybe we'll head back to Lizard's Tongue, maybe even Star City. Getting too old for this life."

"Yeah, well, things are about to change on Epsilon. Come to the meeting tomorrow."

He turned and walked toward the entrance of the massive trunk that contained the elevator. He was suddenly quite tired and wanted nothing but a few hours of rest.

But rest would still have to wait. As it happened he looked up into the sky, past the giant umbrellas and saw something that made his heart stop. He only had a quick glimpse of the tear-shaped vessel but it had been enough.

"Grab your flash rifles," he shouted to the others, "and follow me. You're about to get first-hand experience of what is coming our way." He didn't wait for them and began running in the direction of the cleared area.

When he emerged from the jungle, he saw the alien vessel circling above the small personal habitats that surrounded the open space they used for training newly captured Boraz. He didn't leave the protection of the smaller mushrooms and held back the others who were following him closely.

"What the Hell is that?" one of them asked breathlessly.

"That craft belongs to the Spiders," Turner said.

"What do you mean?"

"It means we have Spiders interested in Epsilon. I can't go into details now. Just trust me on this." Turner watched the vessel stop and hover. A bright flash emerged from its bottom and hit one of the habitats. He watched in horror as the energy beam left a gaping hole in the top of the structure. The vessel targeted two more habitats then it shot back up into the air and disappeared over the mushroom tops.

Turner and the others ran toward the damaged habitats. Turner's fears proved to be unfounded when they didn't find anyone inside them.

"What kind of weapon does this kind of damage?" a prospector asked as they inspected the large holes. "I thought nothing could touch this stuff."

"Nothing we know about," Turner growled. "But now we know better." He remembered how the Spiders had cut the Rex into pieces in a short time. "The Spiders have superior weapons," he said slowly.

Among other things. He thought of Mirna and her ability to influence minds. Even the Reptilians who manned the aircraft they just saw had the ability. He became aware again of the fact Humans didn't know anything about the Spider race. Did all the Spiders have that ability? Or were there only special groups who possessed these powers?

Humans and Spiders were about to go head to head, he had no doubts about that. The Spiders wanted the eggs their ancestors stashed away on Epsilon a hundred thousand years ago. They also wanted to recover the technology hidden in the caves below.

He scanned the sky above them, but there was no sign of the Spider vessel.

"Looks like their gone," he said, wondering if they'd be back. He also wondered if Mirna had been a passenger in that one. Did she know he was here? Had he inadvertently led her to Raptor's Tooth?

"I'm going home," he said. This last run had sapped him of the little energy still left in him. He walked slowly, carrying his rifle in his hand. The pack on his back seemed suddenly heavy and cumbersome and he wanted nothing more than to take it off. As tired as he was, his eyes kept roaming his surroundings and his ears listened to the sounds in the air. On Epsilon one never relaxed. At least not in the jungle.

He stepped onto the elevator and rode it up into the hive. His room lay on the third floor. He took his time getting there. No reason to hurry. There was safety inside the hive, something he hadn't experienced for a long time. Even though he had been safe in the hive of the Queel, and even inside the hive of the Uur, nothing could compare with being back with his own kind. Sometimes he wondered why he bothered to go on these exploration trips. Why did he put himself in danger when he could just stay in Raptor's Tooth and relax? There was plenty of food everywhere. It grew on the shrubs, on the mushrooms, in the ground, as long as one knew where to look for it. But he didn't have to search his mind for reasons. He knew why he did it.

The thirst for adventure was something he could not quell. Boredom was another good reason. Perhaps if he had a good woman by his side he might even decide to settle down and live a more peaceful life. He remembered Geraldine. She had been a good woman, not the most beautiful but certainly one of the more passionate ones he ever met. However, not a faithful one. Thinking of her made him wonder what she was up to right now. Was she still together with that prospector she shacked up with when he was gone? Was she still alive? Women had a tendency to die early on Epsilon, especially the ones who decided to follow the prospectors and fortune hunters into the wild frontier camps.

He never forgot his purpose for coming to Epsilon. He wasn't here to find a fortune or roam the jungle. His real reason had been to collect information, to bring the truth to the High Senate and to expose the Trading Commission for what it really was…a private company, not part of the Solar Union government. He was a spy for the PIA, the Planetary Intelligence Agency.

Things hadn't worked out as planned. He was stuck in the frontiers, unable to convey his information to the PIA. What irony! He had no way to leave Epsilon. The very thing he needed to expose kept him prisoner of this friggen planet. All the wealth buried in the ground didn't help him to purchase a ticket back home. He didn't even have any means to contact another agent because there was no other agent. He was on his own. The only one of his kind. A secret agent. If it weren't so tragic he would almost think it was funny.

The door to his apartment was locked. He put his hand against the plate in the center of the door. When the lock recognized his handprint, it clicked into the open position. He pushed the door into the room and entered.

It was good to be in familiar surroundings. He was hungry but having been away for a long time there was of course no food in his food storage locker. Food would have to wait until morning. He dropped his belongings onto the hard floor and undressed.

* * * *

The last thing he remembered when he awoke was flopping onto his bed. He became aware of a loud pounding and reached for his flash rifle, which lay beside his bed, but then he realized he was in the safety of his apartment in Raptor's Tooth and relaxed. Someone was pounding against his door from the outside with more urgency and then he heard a voice calling his name.

"Turner, open up!"

"All right, all right," he croaked, still sleepy and tired. He looked at his watch and noted he had slept only about four hours.

I wonder what's so urgent to wake me up. Rubbing the sleep from his eyes, he went to open the door. *Amazing how your body reacts when you're feeling safe. I could never sleep like this outside, no matter how secure my hiding place.* Opening the door, he peered at the man standing in the corridor.

"I thought you died in there," the man said.

"Maybe I have and this is just a dream," Turner growled. "Hey, Faulkner, what's the big emergency?"

"I'm happy to see you too, old friend." Faulkner peered up at him. He was even shorter than Turner, who stood only about five foot six inches. "I think you'd wanna come and see this. That ship you and Sinclair saw earlier…well, it came back. Actually, there were two ships." Faulkner didn't comment on the fact Turner was naked. It was nothing unusual in Raptor's Tooth to walk around nude in one's own apartment.

"What? Where are they?"

Faulkner grimaced. "They're gone now. Who the Hell are those people? They killed Ludwig and Vincini, one of the new guys. We got there too late."

"What did they look like?" Turner asked, even though he was sure he already knew the answer.

"Dragons. Never seen any of their kind before. Their skin was sort of green and they had fins coming out of their heads. Didn't wear nothing on top either. Most of them were women, but there were a couple of males with them…from what I saw." Faulkner shook himself. "It looked like they were gonna eat them. Silverstone got his arm chewed up badly. He might even lose it. We shot at them but I don't know if we hit any. Frisky said we hit one. We were still too far away and they got back into their ship before we could get closer."

"Damn!" Turner cursed. "I wonder how they found us." He may have led them here, but he didn't think they discovered the camp because of him. Mirna lost her contact with him before he was taken to the Queel hive. Of course, he gave them some information when he first encountered them. So, in a sense, he was to blame for this.

"Sinclair says you want to have a meeting?" Faulkner asked.

"Yes, that's what I said."

"So you know what's going on? Is that it, Turner?"

He nodded. "Things are happening, Faulkner. This is just the beginning."

"The beginning of what?"

"The war with the Spiders."

"But those weren't Spiders, dammit!" Faulkner stared at Turner. "Have you lost your mind out there? I told you, they were Dragons."

"On the outside, my friend. Only on the outside."

Faulkner shook his head. "I have no idea what you're talking about. It doesn't make sense."

"Don't worry, it will. This is big, Faulkner. I hope we can handle it. I'll explain everything tomorrow at the meeting." He looked at his wristwatch. "No sense to go back to sleep now. I'm hungry. You want to join me at Izabel's for supper? She's still around, I hope?"

"Yes, she's still there. Got herself a partner. Martina. Ugly as sin but a good cook." Faulkner grinned. "I hear she screws like a horny Cricket."

"I didn't know Crickets were horny." Turner smiled despite the gravity of the situation with the Spiders.

"Well, this one is. She even looks like one…sort of." Faulkner punched Turner on the shoulder. "It's good to see you back. Maybe next time you and me go out together. We could take Sinclair along. You know what they say…there is safety in numbers."

"Sinclair told me he and Johnston found some good stuff. They're planning to go back to Epsilon City. Getting too old he said."

Faulkner waved it off with a sweep of his hand. "They've been talking about going back for the last couple of years now. That's all it is…talk."

"Any plans may have to wait until we can get this thing with the Spiders sorted out," Turner said. "If we can sort it out."

"Well, I'm curious to hear what you have to tell us. I also want to hear your story about the Queel who brought you here. I wouldn't have believed it if it weren't Sinclair who told me about it. Is it true?"

"Sure is. I've made some friends. We may need them. Come on in and let me get dressed. Then we'll have supper."

"Do you want to go and see what those Dragons did?"

"No. I'll take your word for it."

Isabel's place was on the next level. She called it *The Big Rex*. It was the only place in Raptor's Tooth where the prospectors who didn't feel like cooking meals could get some descent food. The woman was not young. Too old to work as a *Girl of the Night*, she decided to open up a restaurant. And business was good. Turner didn't remember ever having gone there without finding the place nearly filled to capacity.

The prospectors paid her with gems and some even with money. Others paid their bills with foodstuffs they harvested in the jungle. Fungus, Tubers, fruit…all were welcome. She had a small garden on top of the mushroom umbrella, which was tended by an old prospector who had lost his hand to a reptile and was only too happy to work for food.

"Old Sirhuis still planting lettuce?" Turner asked.

"Yes, he's still digging Isabel's garden. He's also looking after the cistern and the water supply. They finished running the pipes down to the third floor while you were gone. And somebody fixed the pump from the well. No more carrying up drinking water with the elevator." Faulkner chuckled. "Pretty soon everyone will want to live in Raptor's Tooth. We'll be the next big city."

They had arrived at *The Big Rex* and walked into the restaurant. As usual, most of the tables were taken, but they still found one in the back. A couple of minisuns lit up the place quite nicely, but still left a cozy atmosphere. This would be a good place to come with a woman. Turner smiled at the thought. Here he was stuck with good old Faulkner. Not quite the same. Spreeh would have been nicer company.

"What are you grinning about?" Faulkner asked as he lowered his chunky body into the seat.

"Nothing important." Turner looked around the room. The majority of the patrons were men. He saw only the odd woman. He didn't know everyone, but most of them he knew from sight, some by name. Prospectors were on the whole not sociable creatures. They tended to stay by themselves, like Turner. He was only thirty-two standard years old but he had lived alone nearly four years, much of the time in the jungle, away from people and civilization. It was easy, almost natural, to become a loner.

"What are you going to have?"

He looked up at the woman who had approached their table. Faulkner's assessment of her was true…she was no beauty. Actually, downright ugly. Nice body, though. She was younger than he expected.

As horny as a cricket.

She misread his grin and gave him a wink. "I'm free after eight." She smiled and moved her pelvis in a suggestive gesture. "I haven't seen you in here before. Are you new to Raptor's Tooth?"

"Just came back from a long trip. You're new."

"Been here a couple of months now. Still trying to get used to the place. I've made quite a few friends already but there is always room for another one." She gave him another wink. "If you're interested…like I said, I'm free after eight. My name is Martina."

"Maybe another time, Martina," he said, "I need to recuperate from my excursion."

"Did you get lucky?"

"Yes and no. I found some things I wish I hadn't. Come to the meeting tomorrow afternoon. It concerns you also."

"Sounds interesting. Maybe I'll come if I'm free. Now...what can I get you? You want the Special?"

"Sure, whatever it is. I haven't had a descent meal for awhile."

"And you?" She looked at Faulkner who had watched her silently.

"I'll have the same," he said, staring at her ample breasts.

She saw his look and smiled, exposing crooked teeth. "If you want to see more it'll cost you."

He shook his head, scratching his chin. "Don't tempt me, girl. You don't know what monster you might unleash."

"I wouldn't worry about that. I can handle any monster you unleash." Laughing, she walked away, hips swinging.

Faulkner drummed his fingers on the tabletop. "She may be ugly, but she sure knows how to move that ass of hers. One of these days..."

Turner grinned. "If she's as horny as you say, she'll kill you."

* * * *

In the morning, he went back to *The Big Rex* for breakfast. Martina smiled at him when she saw him. "Well, good morning. Nice to see you up this early."

He returned the smile. "Good morning, Martina. I'm not a late-sleeper. When you're on the trail you get up with the sun. What are you offering this morning?"

The corners of her lips turned up in a teasing smile. "Not what I'm offering in the evening. You'll have to wait for that till tonight."

"Tonight I might have to attend another meeting. Like I said yesterday, you should come to the one in the afternoon."

"I'll see if nothing else comes up." She giggled merrily. "Now, for breakfast...how about a couple of fried Moth-Eggs with boiled tubers and a cup of Fernapple juice?"

"Sounds tempting. Sure, I'll go for that."

"Good, because that's all we're serving this morning."

"That's what you're serving every morning," someone said behind Turner.

He looked back and smiled at the man. "Hey, Sinclair. Take a load of those skinny legs." He indicated the chair opposite from him.

The older prospector accepted his invitation. Before he made himself comfortable, he said to Martina, "Might as well bring me the same." He gave her a little wink and watched her walking away. Then he eyed Turner with a frown on his face. "I hear you've talked to Faulkner, which means you are aware of what happened yesterday. If you know what's going on I'd like to hear it. You're arrival here…carried by those intelligent bees in that contraption…it piques my curiosity. And now this unprovoked attack by a bunch of Reptilians? What the Hell is happening here?"

Turner reached into his pocket and pulled out his little camera. "I haven't shown this to anyone yet, so keep it to yourself, okay? I don't want rumors getting ahead of my speech." He flicked on the device but didn't turn on the hologram function to avoid others seeing what he showed Sinclair. "Look at these images."

Sinclair stared at the small screen. "What the…that looks like a habitat. Nothing like ours, though. What is it?"

"It's a habitat. The Spiders built it…in record time, I might add. Our Builder-ships can learn from them."

"What's it doing here on Epsilon?"

"I will talk about that at the meeting." He stared into the other man's lined face, his expression grim. "We are confronted by great danger, Sinclair. The fate of this world may be at stake. The Spiders are claiming it and from what I can see they have a right to do so. They were here long before us Humans, much longer than we can imagine. We cannot justify our presence, but they can."

"What is this talk about Spiders, Turner? I'm confused. Our camp was not attacked by Spiders. They were Dragons, not Spiders. I was there. I saw them."

"They may have looked like Reptilians, on the outside. Inside they were Spiders."

"Are you talking about avatars?"

Turner shook his head. "Not avatars. The creatures you saw were artificially bred to look reptilian. Their minds were Spiders. Believe me, I met them personally. And they have special mental powers. That is the most frightening thing."

"You mean they can read minds?"

"Not as far as I know. What they can do is much more dangerous. They have the ability to take over your mind and body, force you to do things you don't want to do. The females anyway. I don't know about the males."

And some things you want to do, even if it kills you. You look forward to that feeling of euphoria when she punctures your vein with her fangs to drink your blood because she gives you pleasure beyond imagination.

The mental image of Mirna took shape in his mind. He knew she would haunt his dreams and his waking moments for a long time. Her alien beauty had been intoxicating, her passion incomparable.

"Why did they kill Ludwig and Vincini? What was the purpose of that?" Sinclair asked, breaking into his thoughts.

"How were they killed?"

"Their blood was drained out of their bodies. Those Reptilians sucked it out of them." Sinclair cursed under his breath, "Fucken vampires!"

"It's in their nature," Turner said softly. "They were created that way. Don't ask me why." His eyes studied the other man. "Is there by any chance something else you forgot to tell me?"

Sinclair gave him a surprised look. "You mean you don't know? Didn't Faulkner tell you?"

"Tell me what?"

"Those vampires fucked them while they sucked their blood." He cursed again. "What kind of fucking shit is that?"

"That's another thing they do and they do it well. One more way to control you," Turner said with a sour voice.

Sinclair's eyes were large with sudden comprehension. "That's what happened to you, didn't it?" He leaned back in his seat. "You poor bastard. I'm beginning to understand what you went through." His voice sounded sympathetic. "How you must hate them."

"I don't hate them," Turner said, his thoughts far away. "I fear them and what they represent. There was only one female I had sexual contact with, and it bothers me that I literally craved for her embrace and her attention. Still do. She controlled my body and my soul, and there was nothing I could do."

"But you did get away."

"Barely. Were it not for the help of the Queel I would not have made it."

"That is another mystery that's baffling me. I saw you arrive here carried by those giant bees. How the Hell did you persuade them to bring you here?"

"I didn't have to persuade them. They rescued me and offered their help. They want to have positive relations with us Humans." Turner smiled, fondly remembering Spreeh. His relationship with her had been more than just positive; with one important difference...she did not manipulate his emotions and his mind, not the way Mirna had done. Neither had she taken over his body. Sex with her had been voluntary on his part, not forced.

"Why do they want to do that?" Sinclair asked.

"Because they understand things are going to change on Epsilon and they want to defend their world." Turner shrugged. "I guess they like us better than whoever else may lay claim to this planet. They realize that we don't mean them any harm. We are the best alternative they have."

"Let's hope they don't make a mistake. We Humans are not exactly famous for being charitable to indigenous populations, starting with our own planet Earth," Sinclair said, sounding embittered.

"Meaning?" Turner wondered.

"Well, since you were born on an asteroid you probably don't know or even care about Earth's history. My ancestors roamed the prairies on the North American continent long time before Europeans came to invade it. Most of what happened has been recorded in the history books from the side of the trespassers, the winners of the battles between the original inhabitants and the invaders. In other words...the records are tainted. However, the real stories are kept alive and saved from one generation to the next. Not to stir up hatred but to let future generations know the truth. Perhaps some day when we have more time I will tell you some of these stories. Not all of them are pretty." Sinclair looked up as Martina brought their breakfast. "Did you have to dig up those Moth-Eggs?"

"Sorry, it took so long," she said, "but we're extremely busy this morning." Her face looked sullen. "And don't be so grumpy, Sinclair. It doesn't help the mood. Everyone seems so gloomy today."

"They'll be even gloomier tomorrow after they hear what I have to report this afternoon," Turner said.

"One more reason not to come then. I can do without depressing reports," Martina said as she walked away.

Turner and Sinclair ate in silence. Neither of them felt like talking. When they were done eating, Sinclair said, "I'll see you later, Turner. Maybe things won't be so bad."

"Maybe they'll be worse," Turner said.

* * * *

He spent the rest of the day cleaning up his small apartment. When he emptied his pack and took out the sapphires he also found the black crystal spheres. He picked one up and studied it. Hard to believe this was actually an egg. Inside the hard shell slept a young Spider in suspended animation. It was over one hundred thousand years old.

They could not allow the eggs to hatch. The emerging young Spiders would be from a completely different time, a time more primitive and feral. Even though the Spider race had been technically far advanced already a hundred thousand years ago, their minds were not the same. A thousand centuries is a long time for a race to evolve. Nobody knew how those young Spiders would behave. Would they be peace-loving or warlike?

And what about those robotic war machines? What if they were unleashed on this planet against the Humans living on Epsilon or even against the native population? That needed to be prevented at all costs.

The information he had was vital and it was his duty to make certain it reached the appropriate authorities. He faced only one problem. Epsilon had no central government and no military force to protect its population or interests. The Trading Commission was only interested in exploiting Epsilon's resources. The Solar Union's governor, who was also the Chief of the original Scout-Outpost, had no real powers, and yet, he was probably the person who should be made aware of the menace threatening Epsilon, and possibly the whole human race.

Having made up his mind, he decided to go and talk to Stiller, the man who was responsible for the only transmitter in Raptor's Tooth.

Stiller was in his apartment tinkering with the transmitter. "I haven't used this damn thing in ages." He peered at Turner. "I was about to send a message to Lizard's Tongue and report the attack on our camp. I'm not sure it would do any good except for keeping anyone from coming up here. Who's going to help us? Certainly not those bloodsuckers in the Trading Commission."

"What's wrong with the transmitter?"

Stiller shrugged. "No idea. I don't know if I can fix it. I don't have any spare parts."

"Too bad." Turner's hopes were dashed with Stiller's prognosis. The future of Epsilon certainly appeared gloomy and there was nothing they could do to prevent the Spiders from hatching those eggs. "Are you coming to the meeting later?" he asked.

"I'm not sure I want to hear more discouraging news," Stiller said.

"It's important for everyone to know what we're facing. Maybe somebody will come up with a suggestion what we can do. I hope you'll come."

He left Stiller's place with a sinking feeling. With the transmitter out of action, there was no other way but sending a team to Lizard's Tongue to deliver the message. No one would want to travel alone for fear of being attacked by a pack of Raptors or even one of the larger carnosaurs. Only in large groups was there a certain amount of safety. But now with the threat of those alien shuttles volunteers would be hard to find.

He looked at his watch and realized it was time to head for the meeting hall. When he walked in, he was surprised and happy to see the large crowd already assembled. It was obvious that people were concerned and eager to hear what he had to say.

Faulkner was standing and talking in the front of the crowd. He spotted Turner the moment he walked into the room and gave him a quick wave. As Turner walked to the front to join him he caught Faulkner's words, "...Perhaps the arrival of the Trooper means that the rest of Epsilon has experienced similar attacks. We will ask him later, but first I'd like you to listen to someone who just came back from a bizarre and frightening journey. He has a remarkable tale to tell. His unusual return to Raptor's Tooth and the attack on our camp leave no doubt he is speaking the truth. I urge you all to listen to what he has to tell us. Please, welcome my good friend Gilbert Turner."

Turner didn't know what Faulkner's remark about the Trooper meant, but he realized he came just in time. He knew people had been waiting for him.

Clearing his throat, he said, "Thank you, Gerald, for the introduction." He looked at the crowd. "And thank you for coming. You all know about the attack yesterday and are probably wondering what is going on. What I have to tell you..."

* * * *

They were silent after his speech. It seemed most of them were too shocked to even ask questions. He told his audience all the things he thought were relevant. The only thing he didn't tell them was his sexual relationship with Mirna. He only hinted at what she and her reptilian companions were capable of. He also left out many of the details about the Queel and Uur, especially his sexual escapades.

His eyes roamed over the gathered prospectors and fell on the Trooper in the back. He also noticed the two Scouts sitting beside him. Looking at the Trooper, he said, "Gerald Faulkner already acknowledged your presence, Trooper, and he mentioned he would ask you later why you are here. Perhaps now is the time to ask you that question. Do you mind coming up here so we can all hear what you have to say?"

The Trooper rose and came forward. As he came close, he towered over Turner for a moment. Then he turned to face the eager crowd. His expression was grim as he looked into their curious eyes. "I won't make a long speech," he said with a harsh voice. "I listened to this man's report and it only confirms our suspicions about the Spiders. Living up here in this place you call Raptor's Tooth, you are probably not aware that Epsilon has been put under Marshall Law by the Solar Union Space Navy."

He made a short pause to let his words sink in. "This means that the Military decides what happens on Epsilon. As the sole representative of the Space Navy here I am henceforth the Law in Raptor's Tooth. Anything you know about the enemy has to be reported to me."

"What is the Military doing to protect us?" one prospector demanded.

"The Union has sent the *Jupiter*, a Class seven Dreadnought, to this solar system for your protection. Two hundred highly trained Union Troopers are already on Epsilon, also for your protection. There is no need for panic. We have the situation under control and we will defeat our enemy." He spoke with a commanding voice and Turner almost believed him.

Almost.

"I wouldn't underestimate the Spiders," he cautioned. "Their technology is older than humankind and their weapons probably superior to ours."

The Trooper glared at him. "That is subversive talk, sir. You will be briefed later in private."

"I already told you everything," Turner said, irritated by the Trooper's attitude. He was big and imposing and a bully as far as Turner was concerned. His black uniform, the large sidearm and the oversized flash rifle he carried over his shoulder were all designed to intimidate. It didn't impress Turner. He had faced and defeated the Tyrannosaurus Rex, the king of the dinosaurs. A Union Trooper, no matter how large, did not inspire awe in him.

"People never tell everything," the Trooper said, showing his teeth in an almost friendly smile. "You'd be surprised how much additional information you will remember when you're interrogated."

"There are certain things irrelevant to the story."

"Nothing is ever irrelevant. The minutest detail may supply us with an important clue to what we are dealing with."

Turner wanted to protest about releasing private information, when someone touched him on the shoulder. He turned to look at a young, redheaded woman, who seemed to be beaming with happiness.

She looked familiar but he couldn't place her.

"Gil," she cried out and threw her arms around him.

At first he was shocked by her forwardness and wanted to push her away, but then the truth hit him. He didn't want to believe it. This could not be. She could not be here. Should not be here.

He removed her arms from his neck with gentle force and looked at her. "Tara?" he asked, still not believing.

"Yes, Gil, it's me. I finally found you. You're alive." She took his face between her hands and covered it with kisses.

Laughing, he held her away from him. "Stop it. People might think we're lovers or something."

"They would be right with *or something*, big brother," she laughed under tears. "I couldn't wait for you to finish your report to see you. By the time you were done my whole body was shaking." Her face became serious. "You sure had to go through a lot to make it back alive. I would guess you left out a lot. There is probably much more you haven't told us."

"I'm happy for you to have found each other, but we have more important issues to worry about," the Trooper said beside them.

Turner gave the Trooper an angry stare. "Right now nothing is as important to me as talking to my sister who I haven't seen in five years. I don't know why she is here, but that isn't important either. Not at the moment. I want to spend some time with her."

"I'm afraid your reunion with your sister will have to wait, Mr. Turner. The situation is grave and of utmost urgency. I must inform my commander of what you have told us. We must deal with the Spiders immediately." The Trooper spoke with a hard voice that didn't leave any argument.

Turner knew that he was right. Mirna and the others might decide to mount a more concentrated attack on Raptor's Tooth, and this time they'd probably do more damage than the first time. He looked at his sister and shrugged. "I'll talk to you later, all right? Another hour won't make a difference. Meet me in The Big Rex."

She nodded and smiled. "You are right. But hurry, okay?"

He watched her walking away, still not believing to find her here.

Chapter Nine

The Trooper seemed impatient, as did the two Scouts. Turner had given them the location of the Spider camp, which the Trooper forwarded to his commander, who was supposed to be in Epsilon City.

"How long until we know the operation has been successful?" Turner asked.

Mendez, that was the Trooper's name, gave him an annoyed look. "It takes over an hour for the warplanes to travel. I've transmitted the coordinates of the enemy camp thirty minutes ago. All we can do right now is wait."

"In that case I'm going to talk to my sister," Turner said.

Mendez nodded. "You go right ahead. There is nothing for you to do here anyway. This is a military operation from now on."

Turner walked away and headed for *The Big Rex*. When he walked into the room, Tara looked up from her place at one of the tables and smiled happily. The man who sat across from her also smiled.

Tara jumped up from her seat and gave Turner another hug. She laughed and sobbed at the same time. "I was so worried about you, Gil," she said, kissing him on the cheek. "You don't know what I had to endure to find you."

He let her go and looked at her. "You've matured, little sister," he said.

She laughed. "And you...I don't know what to say. Five years is a long time but you still look the same. A few more lines in your face maybe."

He became serious. "I'm really happy to see you, Tara, but you shouldn't have come. This planet is too dangerous and it is about to become even more volatile."

"I had to come, Gil. We haven't heard from you since you left. We thought you were dead."

"Who is *we*?" He was afraid of the answer.

"Do you have to guess?" She looked into his eyes. "The mission is still alive, Gil," she whispered. "They sent me to either find you or replace you, if necessary."

"Now we may both be stuck here," he said with bitterness.

"No, we won't be. I know where we can find a spaceship that is space worthy. It just lies there for the taking." She looked at her friend who was close enough to hear what they were saying. "Dave can pilot the ship. He wants to get off Epsilon as badly as you and I."

Turner looked at her companion, questions in his eyes.

"Oh, I'm sorry, Gil, this is my friend Dave Houston." She smiled at the man. "Actually we are more than just friends."

Houston rose in his chair and held out a hand. "I'm pleased to meet you, Gil. Like Tara said, it took some doing to find you, but I'm happy we found you alive." He sat back down in his chair and gave Tara a puzzled look. "What ship are you talking about?"

"I was going to tell you but never found the opportunity. Demi told me about it. She can take us there."

"How does she know?" Houston asked.

"She was on it. I'll tell you everything later. For now just know that we have a way off this awful planet."

Turner pulled her away from the table. "This friend of yours, Houston, how do you know you can trust him?" he whispered.

Tara smiled. "He loves me, Gil, and I love him. We are going to get married. He is a good man and I trust him with my life. He would never betray my trust. Don't worry about him, please."

"And who is this Demi you mentioned and where is she?"

"She is the nurse who came with us. She's probably still busy stitching up that man whose arm was chewed up in the attack."

"Okay." Turner looked at his watch. "I'd better get back to the Trooper. I need to know what is happening." He gave her another hug and left.

The three men didn't look happy.

"What happened?" he asked.

"Are you sure those coordinates are right?" Mendez asked.

"Of course I'm sure. I showed you the map. Why?"

"Well, we had two planes searching the area. There is nothing there but jungle. No ships, no habitats. Nothing."

"Impossible. I didn't make up this story. You saw the pictures."

"Yes, we did and I believe you." Mendez stared at the screen of his communicator. It was blank at the moment, but as he stared at it, a face materialized on the screen. The screen expanded, changed into a hologram on top of the communicator, displaying the head and shoulders of the Commodore. It was difficult to judge his size, but for some reason Turner knew the man was big. He was older, his face was lined, his gray hard and uncompromising.

"Trooper Mendez, what is the problem?" His voice was as hard as his eyes.

"I don't know, sir. The prospector still sticks to his story and I have no reason to doubt it. The pictures he showed me don't lie."

"Then we have a bigger problem than I anticipated. There is only one way to find out what the Hell is going on. I'll have one of the planes drop off three Troopers and more weapons. You will take the tank and investigate. And take that prospector with you."

"Yes, sir, Commodore Chelzic." The Trooper saluted smartly.

"Are those two Scouts still with you, Mendez?"

"Yes, sir. They are right here."

"Put Stonewall on!"

Mendez nodded to one of the Scouts, who stepped in the commodore's field of sight. "Yes, Chelzic?"

Even though the image wasn't large, Turner noticed the annoyed look on the Commodore's face. "One of these days you will learn to respect your superiors, Stonewall. I want you and Peters to accompany Trooper Mendez on this mission. I'd send more Troopers but those planes don't have the capacity to carry more than four men. So you and Peters will have to fill in. I hope you're up to it."

"Don't worry, Commodore, we'll play along." Stonewall smiled grimly. "Somebody has to keep your Troopers in check."

"You're not there to keep anyone in check, Stonewall! I'm putting Mendez in charge, understood?" Even over the speakers of the communicator the Commodore's voice sounded like the thunder of doom.

Stonewall gave the Commodore a sloppy salute. "Understood."

"Report your position as soon as you get there, Mendez, so we can get an exact fix. If I haven't heard from you two hours after that I must assume that you and your team have been compromised and I will blanket the whole area with implosion bombs. Good luck." The two words were spoken quieter, almost civil.

Turner did not care too much about those last words. Typical Military. Everything had to be done according to rigid rules and illogical assumptions. What if things didn't run smoothly? That Commodore was going to kill them all.

Mendez looked at Turner. "You heard my commander. You'll be part of this mission. How far did you say this Spider base is from here?"

"About fifty miles by air."

"And on land?

"Depends on how and where we travel. On foot it may be over hundred miles because of the swamps and lakes. On the back of a Boraz we can probably whittle that down to seventy miles." He shrugged. "You take your pick."

"I pick a tank." Mendez smiled thinly. "Swamps and small lakes are no problem."

"Good. Perhaps when this is over I'll buy myself a tank like that. Everything will be much easier then." He sat down on one of the benches. "How soon do we leave? I wouldn't mind getting at least one more night of rest. I just came back yesterday."

"We'll spend the night. I'm expecting three additional Troopers. I hope you can find accommodations for us."

"We'll treat you royally, don't worry." Turner closed his eyes for a moment. He was getting tired. The last few days had taken their toll on his body and mind and he was glad to be able to sleep one more night in the safety of his own place. Tomorrow was another day and he wasn't really looking forward to it.

* * * *

They left early in the morning…the four Troopers, the two Scouts, and Turner. He had never been inside a tank and he was amazed at the ease it traveled through the dense jungle. There were no trails to follow, not with a vehicle this size, but it didn't matter. The wide tracks of the tank made their own trail.

Once they were threatened by one of the smaller cousins of the mighty Rex, but the Trooper who sat in the back used the flash-cannon to eliminate the threat. It sure beat dodging the beast and trying to find a crack in a tree trunk or slide under the filthy roots of an Octopus tree.

When they passed the place where Turner lost his Boraz, he advised caution. "We're about ten miles away from the base," he told them. "We don't know what kind of surveillance system they've set up."

"Advice duly noted," Mendez said. "I will launch a spy-eye."

They traveled on in silence. Mendez watched the monitor in the front. He waited for the report of the spy-eye and it didn't take long before the screen lit up and displayed a picture familiar to Turner.

"I'll be damned," Scout Peters said.

"Well, we are now sure that Turner didn't dream up his adventure," Mendez growled.

If you only knew the whole truth, Trooper. I left out a lot, even in my debriefing. I can hardly believe myself what I experienced. He stared at the screen with mixed emotions. The big ship that brought the Spiders in reptilian form still squatted beside the habitat. Not all of the smaller vessels were there. He could also see the elevator that led underground.

After traveling for about fifteen minutes Mendez stopped the tank. "I suggest we travel on foot from here." He activated the tank's transmitter. The face of Commodore Chelzic appeared on the screen.

"We're in position, Commodore. We have located the Spider Base," Mendez reported. "We're exactly half a mile from the base and will move in on foot."

"I have a fix on your position, Mendez. Good luck and remember…two hours."

The four Troopers put on their battle gear, took their flash rifles, and left the tank. Stonewall and Peters fastened their helmets and grabbed their own rifles. Then they also stepped outside.

Turner was the last one to leave the tank. He felt apprehensive. It was too easy. He didn't believe for one minute the Spiders would leave their base unprotected.

He walked behind Mendez and the two Scouts. The Troopers spread out as they neared the base. After a few minutes Turner didn't see three of them anymore. He hoped they didn't forget to watch the jungle around them. Hungry lizards could appear at any time. They didn't take sides and didn't care about the mission of the Humans.

The sun was beating through the umbrellas and the high humidity made him sweat inside his coverall. The impulse to swat at the insects swarming around him like angry wasps was strong. They didn't land on his skin, repelled by his electronic device, but they were a damn nuisance anyway.

When the small group came to the edge of the jungle, Turner said in a low voice, "Unless you want to be seen I suggest we crawl from here on." He pointed to an outcrop of rocks. "We can hide in there, but after that there is no more hiding."

"Then let's crawl," Mendez said.

It didn't take them long to reach the rocks. Turner crouched behind one of the boulders. "How do you want to proceed from here?" he asked.

"Maybe we should wait until dark," Peters suggested. "We can get close under the cover of darkness."

"Not a good idea," Turner said. "There are too many *Night-hunters* around after dark. You'll never see them until it's too late."

"What do you suggest?"

Turner knew what he was going to propose was probably also not a good idea, but it's all he could think of. "They know me. I can get close without being blown to bits…I hope."

"Okay, and then what?"

"I will talk to them. Explain the situation. Maybe they will listen to reason. I suggest we let them take their eggs. That's what they came for in the first place. We'll give them an ultimatum…take your eggs and pack up. Leave Epsilon."

As he was talking he realized how absurd his idea sounded even in his own ears and he wasn't surprised when Mendez stared at him, an expression of utter amazement and pity on his face and in his stance. "That's your great idea? Did you hear yourself talk?" He threw up his hands in disgust. "Why did I expect a civilian to come up with a reasonable strategy?"

"Actually, I don't think it is such a bad idea," Stonewall said. "In fact, I will accompany Mr. Turner and talk to them myself. There are two Humans with them. Perhaps we can get them to work with us. I'm certain if we explain that we want to resolve this issue peacefully, they will listen to reason. The last thing we want is to start a war with the Spiders, and I'm quite certain they don't want a war either."

"I think the time for talking has long past. What about those people they murdered?" Mendez demanded. "Are we going to let them get away with that unpunished?"

"What do you suggest, Mendez?" Stonewall asked. "Do you have a better idea?"

"Yes. We'll get the tank and go in with weapons blazing. We'll be upon them before they know we are here."

"I doubt that," Turner said. "By the way, I believe the decision has been taken out of our hands. We've been spotted and I can only say I'm not surprised." He stood up and stepped away from the boulder he had been hiding behind, watching Mirna and Yules as they walked calmly toward them.

He took a few steps, his hands held away from his body.

Mirna smiled mischievously. "We didn't expect you to come back, Turner. Did you miss me?"

He didn't smile. "Don't pretend ignorance, Mirna. You know exactly why we are here."

She dropped her friendly act. "You are right, Turner. Did you really think you could approach this base undetected? We've known about your presence long before you left that tank you're hiding in the jungle."

"I would have been disappointed were it otherwise," Turner said.

"What do you want?"

"Talk."

"About what?"

"About you leaving Epsilon."

"There is nothing to talk about, Turner. Our claim on this planet you call Epsilon is older than yours, much older, but we have no interest in it except for recovering what is ours. We will leave when we are ready and not before."

"And when will that be?"

She shrugged. "Possibly years from now."

Turner sighed. "Then you leave us no choice. We will have to use force to make you leave."

Mirna let out an amused laugh. "I don't think you have any idea what you are facing, Human. Our race is an old race. We possess knowledge Humans can only dream about. Our weapons and technology are superior to yours."

"I'm inclined to believe you, but our Military doesn't share my belief. And who knows, they may have reason to be confident. You don't know everything about our military strength either." Turner gave her a thoughtful look, questions in his eyes. "Tell me, why can't this base be spotted from the air?"

"Because it is hidden under a cloaking blanket, just like our ships. That's how we were able to land on Epsilon without being detected. How can you even dream of stopping us? We are the superior race."

"We shot down one of your superior aircraft."

Her jade-colored eyes glowed softly when she looked at him. "I didn't say we are invincible. I said we are superior." She came closer. He felt a sudden familiar pulling in his mind. Her mouth opened to display her needle-thin fangs. "You made a mistake by coming back, Turner," she whispered. "This time I may just empty your veins of your blood." She laughed. "Can you feel the pulsing in you loins? I know you do and you can't resist me. You want me, don't you?"

Her soft voice hypnotized him and her eyes bored into his. He wanted to grab her and throw her to the ground...rip the clothes off her body...feel her naked body against his...

He fought the urge, biting his lips until he could taste his blood. "Bitch!" he cursed.

Her hand touched his cheek. "You cannot fight me," she taunted him.

His body felt heavy, he wanted to call to the others for help, but his throat didn't obey him. She put her lips to his ear and whispered, "I want you to tell your friends to come and join us. Tell them everything is fine and I want to talk with them." Putting her tongue into his ear, she chuckled softly. "Once this is over I promise I will reward you."

The pulsing in his loins seemed to overwhelm him and he fought to keep his sanity, pitching his will against hers, but it was a losing battle. His eyes searched out Yules, looking for help, but Yules just stood there, his eyes empty and his face uninterested. Turner turned slowly and called, "Everything is all right. She wants to talk with you."

"We are unarmed. Tell them to leave their rifles behind. Weapons have no place during peace talks," Mirna said softly.

He repeated her words. Then he watched helplessly, as Mendez, Stonewall, and Peters left the relative safety of the boulders...without their flash rifles and their hands away from their bodies.

The Trooper was the first one to come close. He ignored Mirna and addressed Yules, "Are you speaking for the Spiders?"

Yules shook his head. "No, I'm here only as observer. She's the one you want to talk to."

Mendez gave Mirna a cold look. "Go ahead, talk."

Mirna looked him over and gave him a mocking smile. "I assume you are one of the Union soldiers?"

"Yes, I am."

"Impressive." She reached out and touched his cheek in an intimate gesture.

Shaking his head, Mendez stepped back and reached for his sidearm. "Please, stay back," he said between clenched teeth.

Mirna smiled innocently. "Forgive me. I only wanted to make you feel comfortable by showing you that you have nothing to fear from me. Right Turner? Tell the Trooper that I'm harmless."

Turner swallowed hard. He wanted to shout *Don't trust her* but instead he said, "She's harmless, Trooper Mendez."

"Turner and I are old friends. I would not harm him or his friends," Mirna said. "In fact, I would like to demonstrate our hospitality." She turned and let out a shrill whistling sound.

When Turner looked toward the Spider ship, he watched as three of the reptilian females jumped out and came walking toward them. Their bodies shimmered green in the rays of the sun and he realized that they were completely naked.

His mind screamed *Danger* but his vocal cords did not obey him. He watched helplessly as the females came up to Mendez and the two Scouts.

"What is the purpose of this?" Mendez asked.

"You'll find out in a moment, but before we proceed I want to prove to you that we have the upper hand in these…peace talks." She laughed. "By the way, don't you think you should invite your friends to the party?" She whistled again. "Watch." She pointed toward the jungle.

Turner turned his head to look and was horrified when he saw three of the male Reptilians coming out of the jungle, each of them dragging a body.

"What the Hell!" Mendez shouted, again reaching for his gun, but before he and the Scouts could take defensive action, the females reached out and touched their necks.

Mirna pulled a small device from a pocket. "And now for my next demonstration. May I ask to move your attention to the ship?" She touched the screen of the device.

When Turner looked at the ship, he saw a blinding flash coming from a small tower that had appeared out of the outer shell. A moment later a loud explosion in the jungle made him moan. He didn't have to guess what she had done.

"By the way, that was your tank," Mirna said. "It appears now you have no way of going home. Sorry about that, but it doesn't matter. You won't have use for it after we're done." She laughed merrily. "Now the party can truly begin. Everyone follow me. Come, Yules. Come Turner."

She and Yules walked away and Turner followed her like a trained puppy. The other three men walked behind the reptilian females. Three automatons who would do anything they were asked to do. Even if it meant dying.

Turner saw the rest of the Reptilians spilling out of the ship, waiting and watching. Cursing himself for being so stupid, he put one foot in front of the other, unable to resist her command. He should have known what was going to happen, but he had underestimated Mirna's mental powers.

Sorry, Tara, my dear sister, to do this to you. You've come all this way for nothing. The only thing I managed to achieve is put you in danger.

They never reached the group of Reptilians. A whirring sound in the air made him look up and what he saw put joy and hope into his heart.

The sky above them was suddenly filled with winged beings. His eyes saw scaly warriors similar to the Reptilians who were waiting on the ground, but his mind knew that what he saw was an illusion.

The warriors carried spears. They landed among the Reptilians by the ship and began systematically killing them with their spears. Another group landed in front of Mirna and behind Turner. Soon they were surrounded by the winged warriors who held their spears ready to be plunged into Mirna and the other three females, but for some reason they hesitated.

The ring of warriors parted to let a human-looking winged woman step through. Her wings trailed behind her as she came closer. She smiled, looking at Turner.

"Spreeh," he said, suddenly in command of his voice again. "I did not expect to see you ever again, but you are a welcome sight."

She chuckled softly. "We have a bond, you and I. I could not let you die. Besides…" Her eyes rested on Mirna. "We have a common enemy. It is time we begin defending our world."

Mirna glared at her with cold eyes. "Who is this bitch?"

"I am Spreeh, daughter of the Queel queen," she said haughtily. Then she added, "Bitch!"

Turner felt like laughing out loud, but the situation was too grave for that, so he just chuckled. "Now that introductions are over perhaps we shall continue our peace talks."

"I don't know who you are and where you came from," Mendez addressed Spreeh, "I am Trooper Mendez of the Solar Union Space Navy. Thank you for your help, but I believe it is time for the Military to take over."

"I believe it is time for you to shut up, Mendez, and take a backseat," Stonewall said. "You may have noticed that your so-called superior military powers have done little to help us. Our enemy was defeated by primitive spears, not flash rifles and cannons. I also suggest you get in touch with your commander before he begins bombarding this place." The Scout looked at Turner. "It is obvious you know these people. I'm a bit confused, though. When you told everyone about your experience you mentioned the Queel. I understood they were giant…uh…bees. These people certainly don't look like bees."

"No, they don't." Turner made a bow to Spreeh. *I have not told my people about your mental abilities. I was willing to keep your secret.* He spoke the words in his mind.

She gave him a conspiratorial smile. *Thank you my Human friend. I knew I could trust you. It is best we keep our secret. For a while. Not all Humans are trustworthy.* Then she said to Stonewall, "We are the Queel not giant bees. That, as I understand it, is a label Humans put on us."

Turner knew that she had not spoken those words loud because she had no vocal cords, but the illusion was perfect.

Spreeh looked at Turner again. "What do you want us to do with these?" She pointed at the three reptilian females and at Mirna.

He knew what the right answer should be, but he could not bring himself to commit cold-blooded murder. "Let them live," he said.

"It would be wiser to kill them," Spreeh said.

"Turner is right," Stonewall said, "don't kill them. We need to interrogate them."

"Then they are your prisoners." Spreeh nodded. "I will have my warriors search the hives and make sure there are no other survivors. If we find any we will kill those," she said matter-of-factly.

Remembering Clayton, Turner said, "There is another Human somewhere. Do not kill him."

"We won't kill any Humans, I promise."

"And tell your warriors not to enter the large dome. The creatures inside are not alive. They cannot be killed with spears. We will have to deal with them."

Spreeh turned away and gave a silent command to her warriors. Moments later, the majority of them rose into the air and flew toward the jungle. A small group headed for the Spider ship.

The rest stayed with Spreeh and the Humans. "I understand you have lost your transportation," Spreeh said to Turner.

He nodded. "They destroyed our tank."

"We will take you back to your hive," she said.

Turner looked at the shuttle. Turning to Stonewall, he said, "We can use their shuttle. Do you think we'll have a problem flying it? I've seen the controls and they didn't look familiar."

The big Scout nodded and said, "I'm sure we can figure it out. Trooper Mendez is a smart guy."

"Thank you for your offer," Turner said to Spreeh, "but as you heard we will manage." He walked up to her and looked into her human eyes. *You have haunted my dreams.*

She put her hand on his cheek. *It is this illusionary body that you see in your dreams, not me.* Then she leaned forward and kissed him on the lips. *I shall keep you in my dreams also.*

He held her close then for a moment. *There is one more problem we have. These four females have certain mental powers and I'm afraid they will try to take over our minds again once you are gone. How can we prevent that?*

I will put a command into your minds that will allow you to defend yourself should that happen.

He felt spidery fingers touching his mind, almost like a loving caress. Then the feeling was gone. He let go of Spreeh. She moved out of his embrace and walked over to Stonewall and held out her hand. The

Scout seemed surprised by her gesture but took the offered hand. Turner saw a slight frown cross Stonewall's face, but then he smiled, "I am happy to have met you. Thank you again for your help."

"I hope this is the beginning of a prosperous relationship between the Queel and the Humans," Spreeh said. She moved over to Peters and shook his hand also. Trooper Mendez seemed reluctant at first, obviously not trusting her. Typical soldier attitude. Never trust anyone. But then to Turner's relieve he took the offered hand.

Spreeh came back to Turner. *Take care, Gilbert Turner. The bond between us shall never be broken.* She spread her wings and took to the air. Her escort joined her and they took off with a loud whirring of their great wings.

The other Queel warriors were still searching the ship of the Spiders for survivors. Turner did not want to know how many they found. As he looked to the small ship, he saw a lonely figure walking across the hard ground toward them.

Clayton. He had finally decided to join them. Turner did not know what the man's fate would be. Neither did he know what would happen to Yules, Mirna, and the three surviving Spiders in reptilian bodies.

He was certain of one thing. The war with the Spiders had begun.

THE END